"Can you keep a secret? A big one?" asked Rosemary.

"Well, I can work at it," said Barbara. "You know how women are."

"This is no time to be funny," said Rosemary. "Barby, I'm going to get married!" Rosemary's voice was filled with joy and excitement.

Barbara was stunned into silence. Married? Her sister married? She knew Rosemary had become more sophisticated since she had gone away to college, but she had no idea . . . *married.*

BEVERLY CLEARY grew up in Portland, Oregon, and was graduated from the University of California at Berkeley and the School of Librarianship at the University of Washington in Seattle. She is the author of several award-winning books including *Fifteen, The Luckiest Girl,* and *Jean and Johnny,* all available in Laurel-Leaf editions. Mrs. Cleary currently lives in California with her husband.

Sister

of the

Bride

Beverly Cleary

LAUREL-LEAF BOOKS bring together under a single imprint outstanding works of fiction and nonfiction particularly suitable for young adult readers, both in and out of the classroom. Charles F. Reasoner, Professor Emeritus of Children's Literature and Reading, New York University, is consultant to this series.

Published by
Dell Publishing Co., Inc.
1 Dag Hammarskjold Plaza
New York, New York 10017

Laurel-Leaf Library ® TM 766734,
Dell Publishing Co., Inc.

YOUNG LOVE® is a trademark of DC COMICS, INC.

ISBN: 0-440-97596-4

RL: 6.2

Reprinted by arrangement with William Morrow & Company, Inc.
Printed in the United States of America

First Laurel-Leaf printing—June 1981
Tenth Laurel-Leaf printing—November 1984

I guess this is just one of those days, thought Barbara MacLane on her way home from school one bright afternoon late in April. She was not alone. She was walking beside a boy, a very tall boy, but their thoughts were like those famous parallel lines that lie in the same plane but never meet.

Barbara was mulling over the events of the day. First there was that argument with her brother, because his cat had clawed one of the stuffed animals she kept on her bed. At breakfast her father had lectured her on doing better work in chemistry. Part of the afternoon had been spent in conference with her counselor, who thought she should have her future planned as neatly as an English composition. He was an English teacher, who thought life should have a topic sentence. And now she was being walked home by Tootie Bodger.

Tootie, who was six feet four and played the trombone, had his problems. "Just because I'm tall everybody expects me to do things I don't want to do," he was saying as they walked up the hill. "Like dance with all the tall girls when I don't like to dance. And play basketball. All winter the whole school kept asking me why I didn't turn out for basketball, and when the season was over I thought they would forget it. But no such luck. Today the coach stopped me in the hall and said that next season he wanted to see me come out for practice. He said I was basketball material."

"Why don't you?" asked Barbara automatically. It seemed as if everybody in high school had to be some kind of material. That was what her counselor said she was. College material. He had sat there, tapping his nose with that yellow pencil and telling her she was college material and asking what college she wanted to go to and what she wanted to major in when she got there.

"I don't want to go out for basketball," answered Tootie. "I don't care what they do. Flunk me. Expel me. I am not going to play basketball."

"Why don't you want to?" Barbara was more interested in keeping the conversation alive than in learning the answer. It had been easy enough to tell her counselor where she wanted to go. To the University of California, where her mother and father had gone and where her sister Rosemary was now a freshman.

"Aw, I'm not any good. I'd just fall all over my feet," said Tootie.

"Oh Tootie, you wouldn't either." She felt this was expected of her, but she went right on thinking her own thoughts. Her counselor hadn't thought much of her reason for wanting to go to the University, that was plain. And naturally she couldn't tell him that all she wanted to do, all she had ever wanted to do, was catch up with her sister Rosemary. So she had just said lamely that the one thing she was sure of was that she did not want to major in chemistry, and he had said she had better give some thought to her future. . . .

"Yes, I would," insisted Tootie. "I always fall over my feet. Besides, I never can care that much about getting a ball through a hoop. It seems pretty stupid to me, chasing a ball around just to throw it through a hoop. I'd rather practice my trombone."

They walked awhile in silence. It was too bad, Barbara decided, finally giving her attention to the boy beside her, that everyone expected Tootie to play basketball when he was such a good trombone player. The whole school respected him for his ability to play *The Tiger Rag*. You would think that would be enough. She wished she knew of something to say that would make him feel better, not only because she really wanted him to be happy, but because the walk home would be so much easier if he was more cheerful.

"It's getting so I get the feeling nobody likes me."

"Why, that just isn't true," protested Barbara, again because it was expected of her. "You know it isn't true. Everybody likes you. I like you." She saw at once that this was the wrong thing to say.

"Do you, Barbara?" Tootie asked eagerly. "Do you really like me?"

"Of course I do. You know that," Barbara answered impatiently, feeling that Tootie was insensitive to shades of meaning. There was no way to explain that she liked him to smile at in the hall or to talk to before class and that was all.

"No, you don't," contradicted Tootie, his morale sagging once more. "Not really."

"Yes, I do, Tootie." Barbara spoke without much conviction. This could go on all the rest of the afternoon. The whole trouble was that he liked her so much more than she liked him that she felt uncomfortable when she was with him.

"If you really liked me you'd go to the movies with me Saturday night." Tootie looked straight ahead, waiting for her answer.

"I'm sorry," said Barbara. "I would like to, Tootie, really I would, but Mom said something about Rosemary's coming home Saturday, and she said she was going to ask Aunt Josie and Gramma over. You know how it is. Family dinner and all." They turned up Bar-

bara's street, which was damp and woodsy and
smelled of bay leaves.

"Rosemary only goes to the University over across
the bay," Tootie pointed out. "She comes home all the
time. It isn't as though she goes to Vassar or someplace a long way off." His voice was reproachful as he
ducked to avoid a bay tree that leaned across the sidewalk.

Tootie was quite right. Rosemary came home twice
a month to have the orthodontist look at the retainers
that held her newly straightened teeth in place. Tootie
knew this, because his mother and her mother had
been members of the same club for years.

"I am sorry, Tootie," Barbara said firmly, carefully
hiding her real feelings. She should have offered some
more plausible excuse for not going to the movies
with him. After all, she liked him enough not to want
to hurt his feelings. Someday she would learn. Someday she would be as skillful at this sort of thing as
Rosemary. Lucky Rosemary—eighteen, away at college, free of growing boys.

"O.K., if you don't want to go out with me." Tootie
looked gloomier than ever.

Barbara remained silent to avoid any more you-don't-
like-me-yes-I-do conversation. By now they had
reached her house, an L-shaped white house with
green shutters, set in a clearing at the point where the
pavement stopped looking like a city street and began
to look like a road. Sidewalk and curb ended in a
clump of redwood trees beyond the MacLanes' house,
and there the road began to climb and twist up the
hill.

Barbara paused in front of her walk. "Well, good-
by, Tootie. Thanks for walking home with me." There
was no question of asking him in. Mrs. MacLane, who
described herself as three fifths of a teacher because
she taught English and Social Studies part time in the

junior high school, would not be home yet. She almost always stayed after school to help her slowest students. Neither Barbara nor her sister Rosemary, when she lived at home, was permitted to invite a boy into the house unless one of their parents was home.

"So long," said Tootie, who understood the situation. He brightened slightly. "See you tomorrow." He turned and, hunching his shoulders, plodded back down the street.

Poor old Tootie, thought Barbara as she walked around to the back door and let herself in. If only he would stop being so gloomy about everything. Boost his morale in one spot and it sagged someplace else. It was like trying to pick up a handful of cold spaghetti. She stepped into the kitchen, where she found her thirteen-year-old brother Gordy eating cold pork and beans out of a can. His cross-eyed Siamese cat, Buster, was sitting at his feet looking elegant and disdainful even while begging.

"Hi," said Gordy with his mouth full. "I saw old Tootie Bodger walking home with you."

"M-hm." Barbara was not going to admit to Gordy that she was not particularly glad to have Tootie walk home with her, that she considered it a waste of a beautiful spring afternoon. She found the sight of her brother eating cold beans particularly irritating after her exasperating conversation with Tootie. Maybe all boys were exasperating. Maybe this was one of the fundamental truths of life her father was always telling her she had so much to learn about.

Gordy, his red hair uncombed and one side of his sport shirt hanging out, chewed thoughtfully for a moment. "You know, old Tootie even looks like a trombone. Long and narrow."

Barbara wanted to smile, but she would not give her brother this satisfaction. "That's a mean thing to say. He can't help it if he's tall and thin."

Gordy picked one bean out of the can with his fingers and fed it to Buster. "Why a fellow with his build doesn't go out for basketball beats me," he said.

"Tootie doesn't like basketball. He can't see any point in throwing a ball through a hoop," Barbara told her brother. "Can't you put those beans on a plate?"

"Nope. I can't wait that long," said Gordy. He added virtuously, "I'm a growing boy." And he was. He would soon be as tall as his father, whom he resembled. And someday his curly red hair would grow thin and sandy, just as his father's had.

Barbara detected in his manner a certain pleasure in annoying his sister. She and Gordy disagreed about almost everything lately. Their mother said they went out of their way, even took pains, to disagree, but somehow, once they had started differing on every little thing, they could not stop. Neither was willing to let the other have the satisfaction of giving in first.

"I wouldn't call eating cold beans out of a can gracious living," she remarked, feeling that she was one up on Gordy because she knew where her mother had hidden a lemon meringue pie.

"O.K., Miss Barbed Wire, nobody asked you to," said Gordy, picking out another bean for Buster, the cat he had saved his own money to buy.

As much as she disliked being called Barbed Wire, Barbara made up her mind to ignore this brotherly remark. She noticed that the grocery list had been removed from the bulletin board on the cupboard door, and concluded that her mother was going to shop on her way home from school. Probably to buy more cans of pork and beans, thought Barbara as she left the kitchen and carried her books down the hall to the room she shared with her sister Rosemary on the weekends Rosemary came home from college. Mrs. Mac-Lane always watched for specials on anything that would help fill up Gordy when he came home from school. Pork and beans, eight cans for a dollar, were a good buy. So were tamales, four cans for thirty-nine cents.

Barbara opened the door to the bedroom, which was always kept shut to prevent Buster from using her collection of stuffed toys for sparring partners. Now she tossed her books down beside her nineteen animals—the teddy bear, Pooh Bear, Tigger, the stuffed penguin, the fat pink pig and all the rest—which bore snags and tears from Buster's teeth and claws, like wounds from a one-sided battle.

Barbara unbuttoned the pink blouse that Rosemary had discarded after her first semester of college when she took to wearing grays and beiges. If she changed now, she could wear it to school another day and save ironing a fresh blouse. Of course Rosemary, in spite of their mother's protests, was quite right about neutral colors being so much smarter than pastels. But Barbara still thought it was a pretty blouse and was happy to have inherited it along with several other discards that Rosemary did not consider appropriate for college, even though several of them bore good labels. Rosemary had done a lot of baby-sitting to earn those labels.

As Barbara changed into a cotton dress she discovered that she had somehow absorbed some of Tootie's gloom. Lucky Rosemary, who was across the bay at the University and who even owned a sophisticated basic black dress. Rosemary always got to do everything first. Lipstick, heels, dates—always Rosemary was first, and by the time Barbara caught up and was wearing lipstick and high heels on special occasions and being walked home by Tootie Bodger, there was Rosemary way ahead of her in basic black with earrings.

Barbara could never get over the feeling of being a little behind, a little left out. These feelings were intensified on the weekends Rosemary came home from college to share with the family her enthusiasm for her life across the bay. Rosemary seemed so sure of herself. She was even sure she wanted to be a nursery-school teacher, and was looking forward to the work she would do at the University's Institute of Child Welfare. Her conversation seemed sophisticated, full as it was of references to work shifts in the co-operative dormitory where she lived, to mid-terms, and to grade-point averages, words that were strange to Barbara's life as a junior at Bayview High. Oh well, thought Barbara to console herself, as she often had ever since the two sisters were little girls, at least I am the one with the naturally curly hair.

Gordy and Buster must have finished the can of pork and beans, because in the next room Gordy began to play his guitar and sing, "Michael, row the boat ashore. Hallelujah!" Barbara closed her bedroom door. Gordy had been practicing that song for days, and he never seemed to improve.

Gordy stopped, experimented with a chord, and tried it again. "Michael, row the boat ashore. Hallelujah!" It was not right. He tried once more before he continued. "Jordan's river is deep and wide. Hallelujah!"

Barbara sat down on the bed and put her fingers in her ears. This had been going on for weeks. Gordy and two of his junior-high-school friends had formed a trio to sing folk songs. Their ambition—in a year or two when they were really good—was to make records or, rather, "cut" records, as they were always careful to say, that would sell millions. Other boys not much older had done it. Why shouldn't they?

"Sister, help to trim the sail. Hallelujah!" Barbara heard Gordy singing in spite of her fingers in her ears.

Lucky Rosemary, to be away at college and escape this. Poor Barbara, left behind to endure her brother's folk singing, uncertain about her future, forbidden to wear earrings. . . .

But sitting on the bed with her fingers in her ears was a dull way to spend an afternoon. Not that Barbara had anything more interesting to do except, of course, study. She could always study, and she supposed she should study even on a sunny April afternoon, because her father, who taught print shop at the high school, was sure to talk with her chemistry teacher one of these days. But she did not feel like studying chemistry. She felt like . . . she did not know what. Running barefoot through fields of daffodils maybe or writing a poem. Certainly not studying chemistry while Gordy plinked at his guitar and sang in the next room. The sound waves from Gordy's record player managed to get past the fingers in Barbara's ears. He was playing a record of *Michael, Row the Boat Ashore* good and loud, so he could catch and try to imitate the chords of the guitar player.

When Barbara took her fingers out of her ears she discovered that the telephone in the kitchen was ringing. This was a welcome sound. The telephone might keep her from studying chemistry on a sunny afternoon just a little while longer. It had rung several times before she was able to reach the kitchen and silence it by saying "Hello?"

"Hello, Barby." It was Rosemary, muffled and breathless, calling from across the bay. "Guess what? I've found someone to take my work shift and I'm coming home this weekend."

This was not unusual. Certainly it was nothing to be so excited about. "You sound funny. Do you have a cold or something?" asked Barbara. Her fib to Tootie had been partially turned into the truth.

"No, I'm calling from a phone booth down at the

corner drugstore. I didn't want to talk on the pay phone in the hall."

This was strange. Rosemary usually made her calls from a pay telephone on a stair landing in Stebbins Hall, where she lived. There was rarely anything private about her conversation. "Why not?" asked Barbara, now picturing her sister in a telephone booth, her golden-red hair shining against its dark walls.

"Look. I can't talk all day. This is a pay phone and I have only twenty cents," said Rosemary. "Just tell Mom I'll be home late Friday afternoon and to please have something besides meat loaf and string beans for supper."

"All right. But why the excitement?" Barbara knew her sister's excitement was caused by something other than her desire for a change from meat loaf and string beans, a once-weekly dormitory menu.

"Can you keep a secret? A big one?" asked Rosemary.

"Well . . . I can work at it," said Barbara. "You know how women are."

"This is no time to be funny," said Rosemary. "Not on my twenty cents."

"I can keep a secret," promised Barbara.

"Barby, I'm going to get married!" Rosemary's voice was filled with joy and excitement.

Barbara was stunned into silence. Married? Her sister married? She knew Rosemary had become more sophisticated since she had gone away to college, but she had no idea . . . *married*. Why, she was only eighteen. She still had bands on her teeth.

"Are you still there?" asked Rosemary.

"Yes, I'm here," said Barbara.

"Then say something," pleaded Rosemary.

"But who are you going to marry?" asked Barbara, wondering if she should have known without asking.

"Greg, of course, silly." Now that she had shared

her secret Rosemary's tone was light, almost gay. "Who else?"

Who else was right. It had been Greg this and Greg that every time Rosemary came home from school since Christmas vacation. Barbara should not have been surprised. But she was surprised. Rosemary had liked so many boys. Or men, as she called them now that she was in college. "You mean you're in love?" Barbara asked.

"Of course I'm in love!" Rosemary's muffled voice was almost singing. "Why didn't anybody ever tell me being in love, really, truly in love, was so wonderful?"

Barbara, who was in no position to answer, knew this question was purely rhetorical.

"My time is up," said Rosemary hurriedly. "Remember it's a secret until I tell Mom and Dad."

Barbara could not let her sister go. "Wait!" she cried desperately. "Borrow some money. Do something, but don't hang up!"

A moment of silence came over the telephone. "All right," agreed Rosemary. "I see a couple of girls I know at the soda fountain. They ought to have twenty cents between them."

"At least tell me when you're going to get married," begged Barbara.

"June."

"*This* June?"

"Of course."

It was too soon. April was almost gone. May, then June. There wasn't much time. "When in June?" persisted Barbara.

"The tenth. That's between spring semester and summer session," explained Rosemary, as if this made everything very clear.

"But what's that got to do with it?" Barbara wanted to know.

"We're going to summer session," said Rosemary.

This was too much for Barbara to comprehend. "When are you going to tell Mom and Dad?"

"That's why I'm coming home this weekend." Rosemary's voice lost its lilt and took on a worried note. "What do you think Dad is going to say?"

"Well . . ." was Barbara's doubtful answer.

"He seemed to like Greg when I brought him home for dinner that time during spring vacation," Rosemary reminded her sister. "Except for that one argument, and I think he was just having fun baiting Greg. At least I hope so."

"Yes. . . ." The family usually liked the boys that Rosemary brought home. They poked fun at some of them, but since Rosemary had gone away to college they had liked most of the boys or, at any rate, had not found anything seriously wrong with them. They had been more critical when she was in high school. "But you know Dad. . . . And Dad might have been serious about that argument. You know how he is about printing."

"I know I know Dad," said Rosemary. "That's what's bothering me."

Speculating on their father's possible reaction disturbed Barbara, too. *Marriage.* Till death do them part. It sounded so permanent. Their father was sure to feel that there was a big difference between asking a boy home to dinner and marrying him. She could not guess what his reaction might be, but she did know that if he disapproved he would not hesitate to say so and say so forcefully. She recalled that once when Rosemary had bought a cotton skirt with *L'amour! L'amour! L'amour!* printed all over it he had made her return it to the store. He said it made her look boy crazy.

"Say something," pleaded Rosemary from across the bay.

"There isn't much I can say," said Barbara. "You know he may go straight through the ceiling."

"I know." There was despair in Rosemary's voice.

"And Mom will say, 'Now, now. Let's talk it over.'" Barbara hoped she was offering some comfort.

"I know," repeated Rosemary. "Well, I guess I'll find out soon enough, and I'll manage Dad somehow. Look, meet me at the bus around five o'clock Friday afternoon, and don't breathe a word to anybody. Promise?"

"I promise," agreed Barbara.

There was a sudden wail from the other end of the line. "Oh-h! They're leaving!" The receiver was slammed onto its hook, and Barbara knew that her sister had dashed out of the telephone booth to borrow twenty cents.

Well. Rosemary engaged to be married. Barbara still could not believe it. Bewildered, she continued to stand with her hand on the telephone. Rosemary married to Greg . . . what was his last name? Aldredge. Dark, slight Greg. That was a bit of a disappointment. Barbara had always pictured both her sister and herself marrying tall men. She searched her mind for every scrap of information about Greg Aldredge. She knew he had originally come from the East, because he had amused the MacLanes by his references to "out here." Out here people were friendlier. Out here people were less conventional. That sort of thing. His family now lived someplace farther down the peninsula below San Francisco. He was a graduate student, majoring in English and minoring in History. No, it was the other way around. His major was history and his minor English. He had a brother who was a pre-med student at the University and a sister who was a Physical Education major. He had an old car, and he had spent two years in the Air Force. This was all the specific information Barbara could summon about Greg. Except, of course, the argument.

Stunned as she was, Barbara could not help smiling as she recalled the talk at the dinner table the evening Rosemary had brought Greg home. Mr. MacLane, whose students printed the yearbook in the˜school print shop, had remarked that the yearbook staff wanted the names under the pictures of the graduating class printed entirely in lower-case type. Mr. Mac-Lane, a man who pretended exasperation with the human race, was particular about capital letters, punctuation, and proper syllabification at the end of a line. Any student who divided Eng-lish into Engl-ish caught it from Mr. MacLane. He was famous for saying, "If you don't know, look it up," to his classes, and this earned him the nickname of Old Look-it-up Mac-Lane. Naturally he was impatient with a yearbook staff that had such a notion as reducing capital letters to lower-case letters.

Greg made the mistake of mentioning the poet E. E. Cummings, who did not use capital letters or punctuation and often ran words together for effect. Of course this provoked an argument from Mr. MacLane. What if every author took it in his head to throw away the rules? What kind of books would we have then? Books that no one would read, that's what we would have. Greg felt that the printer's job was to print the text, not criticize the author's art. Not that he did not respect punctuation, you understand, sir, but. . . . Mr. MacLane had a lot to say about the contribution of the printer to the art of bookmaking, and Greg had been silent or, anyway, had kept still.

"Sister, help to trim the sail. Hallelujah!" Gordy sang with a new chord, bringing Barbara back to the present. Still she did not move. Gay, popular Rosemary washing socks? Impossible. Now why did I think of a thing like that? Barbara asked herself. Mar-

riage was not washing socks. It was love and moon-
light and orange blossoms. Things like that. New
dishes, new clothes, everything brand-new all at once.
Oh, dear, now she would never catch up with Rosemary.

And a wedding, Barbara thought suddenly, meant
bridesmaids, flowers, parties, presents . . . and she
was going to be in on all the fun. The gloom she had
felt after her walk home from school was entirely gone
now. The secret began to well up within her until she
felt as if she would burst if she did not tell someone.

"Jordan's river is deep and wide," sang Gordy. "Hallelujah!"

I won't tell, Barbara reminded herself. I promised.
Cross my heart and hope to die. Unanswered questions flooded her thoughts. Forty cents' worth of telephone conversation had not been nearly enough.
There would be several bridesmaids, of course, with
Barbara, the bride's only sister, as maid of honor in
blue with a nosegay of pink roses. Or perhaps green
with yellow roses. That would become a brown-eyed
blonde. Barbara decided she must start reading the
society pages to find out about these things.

Now in her imagination Barbara, maid of honor,
was coming out of the church on the arm of a college
man, who was attentive to her all during the reception. People were looking at them and smiling and
thinking, What an attractive couple they make. Now
she was waiting with the bridesmaids for Rosemary to
throw her bouquet . . . she was catching it . . .
everyone was smiling and nodding. Of course the maid
of honor would be the next bride.

Just then Mrs. MacLane startled Barbara by opening the back door and carrying in a bag of groceries.
"Help me bring in the rest of the things, will you,
dear? I'm late because I stopped at the Department of
Motor Vehicles to pick up copies of the motor-vehicle

code for my ninth graders. They're all interested in driving cars, and I thought traffic rules might be something that would interest them in reading." Mrs. MacLane taught three classes of slow students, of which the ninth grade English class was the most difficult.

"Sure, Mom." Barbara was surprised that her mother had noticed nothing unusual. Her one thought, Rosemary is going to get married, was so intense she felt it must surely be audible.

"Sister, help to trim the sail!" sang Gordy in a new experimental way that was almost a howl.

"Goodness," remarked Mrs. MacLane, "I should think Sister would have that sail trimmed by now. This has been going on for at least a week."

Barbara was glad to escape the garage to pull a bag of groceries out of the luggage compartment. As she did so, a can of cat food tumbled out and rolled down the driveway. This was Tuesday, she thought as she ran after it. Wednesday, Thursday, and then Friday. She did not see how she could ever keep a secret that long. But she had to. She had promised.

Chapter Two

If the secret within Barbara had been written in music, this part of her day would have been marked *crescendo*. The news seemed gradually to increase in force within her until she felt as if she must shout, "Rosemary is going to get married!" While she set the table for dinner she tried to think of something else—school, her English assignment, Tootie, anything—but her thoughts always flew back to Rosemary and her wedding. A lovely wedding in June, with Barbara as maid of honor catching the bridal bouquet. Oh, joy, oh bliss and a handsome best man, hallelujah, her thoughts sang as she folded the paper napkins in half. April, May, June, here comes the bride, hallelujah!

Mrs. MacLane, who was unpacking groceries in the kitchen, remarked, "The Safeway had another special on pork and beans. It's a good thing Gordy never seems to tire of them. And there was a special on cat food for that cat of his. I do hope Buster won't turn up his nose at this brand."

Beans and cat food. Barbara felt a twinge of pity for her mother as she got out the greens and the wooden bowl and started to prepare the salad. There seemed to be no room in her soul for poetry since the school board, hearing that she had a teaching credential, had prevailed upon her to take over three classes of slow students. But then, of course, her mother did not realize there was going to be a wedding in the family so soon.

Mrs. MacLane began to pack the meat she had bought into the refrigerator, and Buster came running into the kitchen to rub against her legs and purr hoarsely. "Scat," said Mrs. MacLane, and gave Buster a shove with her foot. "Wouldn't it be nice if people purred as charmingly as cats when they are hungry? Half the quarrels in the world would never take place."

"Especially people like Gordy," agreed Barbara.

As if in answer Buster stopped purring, fixed Mrs. MacLane with his crossed blue eyes, and began to swear, as only a Siamese cat can.

"Speaking of Gordy," said Mrs. MacLane, "he'd better feed this cat if I am ever to get dinner on the table. Gordy!" she called above the sound of the record player. "Come and feed your cat, so I can get dinner in peace."

Gordy slouched into the kitchen. His mother looked at the tousled hair, the hanging shirttail, the sneakers without laces, and did not conceal her irritation. "Gordy, can't you pull yourself together? You look so untidy. I don't like to see you look so sloppy."

"Aw, Mom, do you have to pick on me all the time?" Gordy asked. "No matter what I do somebody in this family is always picking on me."

"Gordy, I'm not picking on you!" Mrs. MacLane snapped. "But there is no excuse—"

"Mother, you just said people should purr when they are hungry," Barbara reminded her mother, as she finished the salad. "You'd better start purring."

Mrs. MacLane laughed ruefully, and Barbara felt this was a good time to let her mother have the kitchen to herself. She went into the living room and flopped down on the couch, where she looked critically around the living room and dining room. The wedding would not be here. Rosemary would want to be married over in Woodmont, the next town, in the church the family had attended since Barbara could remember. The towns of this county, the population of which had doubled and redoubled in the past twenty years, were so close together that it was easy enough to drive to the church of one's preference in a few minutes, even though it was in another town. This was what Rosemary would want to do. There was no question about that.

But the reception? The house was less shabby since her mother had gone back to teaching. The carpet was not quite a year old, and a chair had been re-upholstered long enough for the newness to wear off that had made the other chairs look shabby by comparison. It was a comfortable house of no particular style or period. But would Rosemary want the reception here? Barbara wondered. She speculated about the cost of a wedding reception at the country club, even though she knew this was out of the question. Oh well, there was really no point in trying to plan the wedding until Rosemary came home.

Barbara picked up a magazine that was lying on the couch. She tried to read a story, but she was too wedding-minded and the advertisements were too distracting. Pictures of silverware made her wonder which pattern she would choose if she were Rosemary. Finally Barbara settled on a perfectly plain pattern that looked as if it could be inherited from someone's grandmother. It would go well with anything. Next, she selected two kinds of bath towels—plain blue and white, printed with blue roses—co-ordinated, the advertisement said, with sheets and pillowcases, also printed with blue roses. If Barbara were the bride instead of Rosemary she certainly would want to be co-ordinated. She read on. Refrigerators, washing machines, even detergents and scouring pads, took on interest in the light of Rosemary's news. Oh, but Rosemary was going to have fun. All that shopping . . . wedding presents . . . packages to unwrap. Barbara dreamed on until she was called to dinner.

She continued to dream of the wedding through dinner and only half listened to an argument between her father and Gordy. Gordy told his father that he was probably born with a C mind and, in that case, it was senseless to expect him to be an A student. His father pointed out that people who were born with C minds simply had to work harder. They often did better than A minds who wasted their talents. And anyway, Gordy wasn't going to get by with that old C-mind argument in this household. He was a MacLane, wasn't he? That was enough.

Barbara was suddenly aware that she had been so busy daydreaming about the wedding and trying to keep the lid on Rosemary's secret that she had completely forgotten to mention her telephone call. "Oh, by the way," she said, in what she hoped was an off-hand manner, "Rosemary phoned this afternoon. She said to tell you she was coming home Friday for the weekend."

"Just before mid-terms?" Mrs. MacLane expressed surprise. "Her appointment with the dentist isn't until a week from Saturday. Did she say anything else?"

I won't tell, I won't tell, Barbara thought desperately as she said, "She said please don't have meat loaf and string beans for dinner."

"I like meat loaf and string beans," protested Gordy.

"You like anything that will fill you up," his father reminded him.

Who wants to eat meat loaf and string beans when she is in love? Barbara asked herself. Nobody. Love calls for strawberries and angel-food cake and meringue and possibly, for something more filling, cheese soufflé. Fluffy things.

"I know how monotonous dormitory food can be, especially in springtime." Mrs. MacLane, who had attended the University during the depression, sympathized with Rosemary's request. "I remember how I used to long for fresh asparagus and strawberries when it seemed as if we had been living on carrots and bread pudding all winter. I saw some fresh strawberries in the market today. I think we'll have them for a treat when Rosemary comes home, even though they are a little high yet."

Barbara wished her mother had not mentioned the cost of strawberries. She would prefer to have Rosemary eating strawberries, oblivious of the price because she was in love. Sometimes her mother seemed positively earth-bound by the details of living, but then she did not know she had a daughter in love. Not yet. Barbara rose to clear away the dishes and to serve the lemon meringue pie, which her mother had already cut. There were little beads of brown moisture rising from the meringue, causing Barbara to reflect that although her mother was a good-enough cook, she would never be invited to go back East to take part in a Pillsbury bake-off contest.

"I don't think she should come home when she has to study for mid-terms," remarked Mr. MacLane. "I don't care how much meat loaf she has had to eat at school."

"Perhaps she feels she can get more studying done at home," suggested Mrs. MacLane. "Sometimes it's hard to study with a roommate and her friends around all the time. What does surprise me is that she could tear herself away from Greg, the way she talks about him all the time."

Barbara, who had served the pie, now took her place at the table. She was careful to keep her eyes on her pie.

"Who knows? Maybe they've had a fight. Maybe

our daughter is coming home to mend her broken heart," said Mr. MacLane jovially. "You know how kids are."

The family ate the pie with the beady meringue in silence for a few minutes. Barbara tried to think of something to say that was far removed from the subject of Rosemary and Greg, but all she could think of was her walk home with Tootie Bodger, and she was not particularly anxious to mention him. Her mother was always so enthusiastic about Tootie. He was such a nice boy, she said, in spite of that ridiculous nickname. Barbara decided that if she absolutely had to, she would fling Tootie into the conversation to keep her family from asking too many questions about Rosemary, but only as a last desperate measure. She was beginning to feel worn-out from the excitement of her secret. Maybe by now she was too tired even to want to tell it. She hoped so.

People should keep their own secrets, Barbara thought suddenly. Rosemary had not been able to contain her secret and, to relieve her own crescendo feeling, had passed it on to Barbara who, according to the unreasonable rules of secrets, had to contain it or feel that she had betrayed her trust. It was not fair.

"Tom, do you think Rosemary is getting serious about this Greg? Really serious, I mean," Mrs. MacLane suddenly asked her husband. "She has talked about nothing but Greg for months, and now they've been going to museums together. You know that isn't a bit like Rosemary."

Gordy agreed. "A wienie roast is more her speed."

If I were a character in a comedy, I would either choke on my pie or spill my milk, thought Barbara, who did neither, even though she would have liked to distract her parents in some way. Perhaps this was the moment to fling Tootie Bodger into the conversation.

"I hope not," said Mr. MacLane. "She's only eighteen, and she has three more years of college."

"I know . . ." said Mrs. MacLane thoughtfully, "but girls get married younger nowadays. You know that. And a girl as attractive as Rosemary is bound to meet someone sooner or later in such a large school."

"She had better buckle down and bring up her grades if she expects to stay there long enough to meet him," observed Mr. MacLane.

"I wonder if Greg had anything to do with her poor grades last semester," mused Mrs. MacLane. "Or was it the shock of finding herself one of over twenty thousand students after a small high school?"

"She's up against competition that is a lot stiffer than anything she has ever faced before," Mr. MacLane pointed out, as he pulled a cigar out of his shirt pocket and took off the cellophane wrapper. He always settled back and smoked a cigar after dinner, and there was nothing his daughters could do about it. "Besides, why on earth would she want to marry Greg?" he asked in the jovial manner a cigar always evoked. "I doubt if he could support her in the style to which she is accustomed, and that style includes twenty-five dollars a month for the orthodontist. I'm certainly not going to support her after she gets married."

"She won't be wearing bands very much longer," said Mrs. MacLane.

Oh, thought Barbara, nervously rolling the edge of the place mat between her fingers, this is *awful*. Now it was too late to throw in Tootie Bodger to save Rosemary. "I thought Greg was nice," she said, and hoped her remark was not significantly conspicuous.

Mrs. MacLane considered Greg. "For one thing, he is older than Rosemary and has been in the Air Force. I think she finds that attractive."

Mr. MacLane lit his cigar, shook the lighted match, and blew out a puff of smoke. "If it's age she wants, I'm sure she can find someone more decrepit than Greg."

Oh, swell, thought Barbara miserably. Now he was going to start being funny. She was sure of one thing. *Her* husband, if she ever had one, would never smoke cigars. That was qualification number one. Positively no cigar smoking. Qualification number two: be serious about his daughters.

"Barbara, get me an ash tray," Mr. MacLane ordered.

"Sure, Dad." Barbara was glad to leave the table even for a moment. She would have liked to excuse herself altogether, but the conversation had such a horrid fascination she could not bring herself to miss it.

Mr. MacLane accepted the ash tray. "A man's home is his castle," he informed his family. "He has a right to expect ash trays to be handy and salt shakers to be full at all times."

"And never find nylons dripping in the bathroom," prompted Barbara, hoping her father would elaborate on a man's home is his castle. This was a subject that could keep him going as long as his cigar lasted. The vacuum cleaner should never be run while the man of the castle was listening to the ball game. Telephone calls from other girls should not exceed five minutes. Anything worth saying could be said in that length of time. That sort of thing, on and on in a bantering way that had a serious undercurrent.

Mrs. MacLane, however, was not ready to let the subject of Rosemary drop. "I wouldn't like to see her get really serious about a boy when she is only eighteen. It seems so awfully young."

"Rosemary married? That's a laugh." Gordy, having

finished the last crumb of piecrust was ready to join the conversation. "Remember that time she cooked the cucumbers, because she thought they were zucchini? The poor guy would starve to death."

Mr. MacLane leaned back in his chair and exhaled a cloud of blue smoke. "Supposing she is serious about him," he said good-naturedly. "That doesn't guarantee he is serious about her. She'll have to catch him before she can marry him."

Barbara kept her mouth shut tight.

"E. E. Cummings," said Mr. MacLane derisively, and Barbara could see that he was all set for one of those half-jovial, bantering conversations. "I would hate to see any daughter of mine throw herself away on someone who approved of writers who did not use punctuation or capitals. This fellow Greg probably likes *archy and mehitabel*, too."

"So do I, Dad," said Barbara. "And the reason there aren't any capitals in *archy and mehitabel* is that it was supposed to be typed by a cockroach, who couldn't jump on the capital key and a letter key at the same time. The author wasn't just being lazy. He had a good reason."

Mr. MacLane chuckled. "A book written by a cockroach is just about what I would expect this fellow to like."

Barbara laughed in spite of herself.

Mrs. MacLane had ignored this bit of conversation. "I don't know," she said with a sigh. "I wish I did."

Mr. MacLane flicked a little tower of ash from his cigar and smiled. "I wouldn't worry if I were you. Why would anybody want to marry a flighty girl like Rosemary?"

"Dad!" Barbara's exclamation was involuntary. "Is that the way you talk about us behind our backs?"

"All the time," answered her father comfortably.

Barbara sat in injured silence. It was no wonder Gordy was such an exasperating brother. It was hereditary. He had an exasperating father. She wondered what it was like to be some other girl, one with a meek father who agreed to everything and handed out a nice fat allowance.

"Oh, I don't know that Rosemary is completely scatterbrained," said Mrs. MacLane seriously. "She just likes to have a good time, and besides, college students have so much to do I think they sometimes seem to be going in several directions at once. She is really a very well-meaning child." Child, thought Barbara dismally. Rosemary is practically a married woman, and Mother is calling her a child.

"She has never uttered one word of complaint about having to live in a co-operative house at the University. Washing glassware for a hundred girls after dinner every day as her share of the work can't really be a pleasure. She seems to enjoy her life, and so many girls we know would be unhappy if they couldn't live in a sorority house or at least one of the new dormitories."

"Well, I wish she would stop scattering her brains and bring her grades up," said Mr. MacLane. "I think I'll have a talk with her this weekend. Tell her she can't carry fifteen units of studies and another fifteen of this Greg and expect to make the grade."

If her father had begun to talk about Rosemary's grades and Greg at the same time, the moment had come for Barbara to make the sacrifice and throw Tootie Bodger into the conversation. "Tootie Bodger walked home with me today," she announced.

"That's nice," said Mrs. MacLane. "Tootie is such a nice boy."

"I suppose so," said Barbara. Tootie was probably kind to animals, too, but that did not make her want to go to the movies with him.

"He'll probably ask to take you out one of these days." Mrs. MacLane smiled her approval at her younger daughter.

"Maybe," murmured Barbara. Harmless old Tootie— kind to animals, trusted by mothers—Barbara would be only too happy to trade him for a best man or an usher.

"What that boy needs is to turn out for basketball," remarked Mr. MacLane, who not only knew every boy in Bayview High, but had definite opinions about what they should or should not do.

"But he would only fall all over his own feet." Barbara used the words straight from Tootie's mouth and wondered how she got on this side of the argument. Probably because she was talking to her father. For some reason, the last couple of years, she seemed to argue with her father every time she talked to him whether she intended to argue or not. She had not meant to defend Tootie, although she liked him in an impatient sort of way. She even felt a little sorry for him since Gordy had pointed out that he was shaped like a trombone.

"If he learned to handle himself on the basketball court he might stop falling over his feet," Mr. Mac-Lane said.

"But Tootie doesn't want to conform." Barbara knew her father felt there was too much conformity among high-school students. "He doesn't want to be pressured into playing basketball just because he's tall. He wants to play his trombone."

"He could do both," suggested Mr. MacLane, "although not necessarily at the same time."

"You don't understand," said Barbara, ruffled at her father's attempt at humor. "Tootie is dedicated to his trombone. He is *serious* about it. He is studying with a man from the San Francisco Symphony. He just plays *The Tiger Rag* and things like that because the students like it.".

"I don't see why he puts up with a nickname like Tootie," mused Mrs. MacLane.

"He likes it better than his real name," explained Barbara. "How would you feel if you were six feet four and your real name was Robin?"

"I can't imagine what Nancy Bodger was thinking of when she named him Robin. He must have been a fat, pink baby," said Mrs. MacLane, and she patted Barbara's hand. "I'm glad you like him, dear."

Now I've done it, thought Barbara. Just wait until the next Amy meeting.

Mrs. MacLane's club, originally called *L'Ami*, because this was French for friend, had been changed by some irreverent husband, possibly Mr. MacLane, to the Amy Club, and its members were known to their families as the Amys. When the club was formed its purpose had been the raising of funds for worthy causes, but somehow over the years it had gradually become a social club, without officers or dues or even regular meetings, whose chief purpose, as far as Barbara could see, was to be an excuse for its members to get together, eat rich desserts, and talk about their children, usually in a humorous vein. Rosemary and Barbara poked fun at the Amys, and Rosemary said the real trouble with the Amys was that they did not use their minds.

Now Mrs. MacLane and Mrs. Bodger would probably compare notes, conclude that Tootie and Barbara liked one another, and make all sorts of little plans to help them get together. If Barbara did not look out she was going to be stuck with Tootie, all because her father made her feel contrary.

Barbara suppressed a sigh as she rose to clear the table. She could not help feeling noble at the way she had sacrificed herself to help save Rosemary—for the moment. She did not envy her sister the weekend that lay ahead, because she was not sure her father had been entirely joking in his remarks about Rosemary and Greg. He often spoke lightly of matters that he was most serious about.

Mr. MacLane, who had worked with young people so many years, was never intimidated by them, and he never hesitated to speak his mind. It was a real problem. Barbara sometimes felt that life would be easier for her and Rosemary if they had a father who could be moved by persuasion, tears, or sulky silence. Poor Rosemary. She wondered if she should try to telephone her at the dormitory to warn her of what lay ahead, but she decided against it. There would be plenty of time for warnings when she met Rosemary at the Greyhound station. Let Rosemary have a few more days of happiness.

Mr. MacLane had left the table and had settled himself in the living room to enjoy his cigar and his evening paper. Barbara cleared away the last dessert plate, and as she rinsed them under the faucet she wondered how anything as fluffy as meringue, even beady meringue, could become so gluey when it stuck to the plates. Her mood was no longer crescendo. Since her father's remarks about Greg and Rosemary *diminuendo* was a better word. Her excitement was diminished to the point where her secret was going to be easy to keep until Friday. She no longer wanted to tell anybody because, if the dinner-table conversation was any indication, there might not be a wedding at all.

Chapter Three

Barbara's spirits refused to remain diminished. She spent the next few days alternately imagining the trouble Rosemary was going to have with their father and dreaming about the wedding. She wondered what would happen if her father said flatly that Rosemary could not marry Greg. But he couldn't say that, not really, because Rosemary was eighteen. But if he did, and of course he wouldn't—or would he?—it might make a difference in the wedding plans. Maybe Rosemary and Greg would feel they had to elope, and that would spoil all the fun. There wouldn't be any bride's bouquet to catch.

In a happier mood Barbara read the society pages in the newspaper. No wedding story escaped her. Brides in satin, brides in faille, brides in organdy, brides with wreaths, Juliet caps, and cathedral trains, brides in suits—Barbara passed quickly over these unimaginative creatures and went on to brides with nosegays, shower bouquets, or prayer books—there seemed to be no end to the delightful possibilities. And the attendants! Bridesmaids in yellow organza with sprays of gladioli, bridesmaids in turquoise taffeta with daffodils, a single attendant in blue chiffon with a nosegay of garnet roses and carnations.

It all made such lovely springtime reading.

Then Barbara happened upon a description of a slipper-satin wedding gown that had been worn almost ten years before by an older sister, who had been married in the same church. During the interval, the story said, the ivory shade of the dress had deepened to soft gold. This made Barbara stop and think. Being careful with his money as he was, insisting on margarine instead of butter, her father would probably expect her to use the same wedding dress when her turn came—that phrase again! She had spent her whole life waiting for her turn to come—and yellow was her most unbecoming color. She would never want to walk down the aisle in yellow. Somehow she would have to see to it that Rosemary did not choose ivory satin. In fact, if both of them were to wear the same dress, it seemed only fair that they select it together. It would be *their* wedding dress, not just Rosemary's. Our wedding gown, thought Barbara dreamily, and she began to see herself clinging to her father's arm, her eyes lowered, starting down the aisle some hazy day in the far, far distant future.

Friday afternoon at five o'clock Barbara was waiting in front of the Greyhound station when Rosemary got off the bus with a suitcase, an armful of books, and an extra coat over her arm.

"Hi," said Barbara, taking the suitcase because Rosemary would have difficulty carrying it while she was wearing such high heels. "Why such a big suitcase? You still have a toothbrush at home." Unexpectedly she felt a little shy with her older sister. Rosemary, who had begun to change when she went away to college, now seemed almost like a stranger. She was engaged to be married and would not have that extra toothbrush at home much longer. She looked thinner and more sophisticated, although perhaps this was due, as her mother was sure to say, to dormitory food and so much walking on a hilly campus. But whether Rosemary's slim figure was due to sophistication or to diet and exercise, Barbara suddenly felt as if her own skirt was too full and her saddle shoes enormous. She felt like a puppy that had not grown up to its feet.

"The suitcase is full of dirty clothes. Too many to wash by hand and not enough for a load at the Laundromat," explained Rosemary. "I brought the coat home for Mother to shorten. It's so long it practically flaps around my ankles."

Barbara felt better. This sounded more like the old Rosemary. She wondered how her mother would feel about the laundry and the coat to shorten when she had papers to correct and lessons to plan, but she did not say anything.

"How's everybody?" Rosemary asked, avoiding the topic on both their minds.

"Fine. Gordy's still a pain in the neck, but otherwise we're all fine."

Rosemary laughed. "You and Gordy are just suffering from sibling rivalry." Since Rosemary had gone away to college and roomed with a psychology major her conversations were sprinkled with psychology-book phrases.

"You mean we are quibbling siblings?" asked Barbara.

"Something like that." The girls walked in silence until finally Rosemary spoke the question that was on both their minds. "What do you think Dad is going to say when I tell him?"

Barbara became cautious. She did not feel it was her place to repeat the conversation she had heard between her parents about Rosemary and Greg, particularly since she was not sure to what extent her father had been joking. Still, she wanted somehow to warn her sister that he might object. "Shouldn't Greg ask Dad for your hand?" she asked, taking refuge behind a half-joking manner.

"That went out with fans and bustles," said Rosemary. "Greg is coming over tomorrow night to talk to

Dad, but I thought I should break it to him first. What do you think?"

"Well," began Barbara, choosing her words with care, "Mother did wonder if maybe you and Greg were getting serious."

"That's good. Then they shouldn't be too surprised." Rosemary seemed relieved. "What about Dad? What did he say?"

"Oh, you know Dad," answered Barbara as airily as she could under the circumstances.

"That's the trouble," said Rosemary. "He must have said something. Come on, what was it?"

"I . . . I don't remember exactly," lied Barbara. "Some silly remark about your cooking or something. And he did mention your grades."

"Oh." Rosemary put a lot of expression into that one syllable. Comprehension, disappointment, apprehension. She laughed nervously. "Well, I guess it was a good thing I had to give a debate in high school. Maybe it will help now."

"Did you win?" asked Barbara tactlessly.

"No," sighed Rosemary, "but I was trying to prove that a twelve-month school year would be better than a nine-month year. It was pretty hopeless."

Barbara shifted the suitcase from her right hand to her left hand and back again. The pecking of Rosemary's heels on the sidewalk was the only sound until she said, "Maybe things really were better back in the days when a man had to ask a girl's father for her hand in marriage."

At home Rosemary spent the time before dinner at her desk, alternately staring into space and trying to concentrate on her French with her fingers in her ears while Gordy sang "I've got twenty-nine links of chain around my leg" in the next room. Dinner at the Mac-Lanes' that evening was pleasant enough, even though Barbara and Rosemary tried to conceal their nervousness. Rosemary appreciated a change from dormitory diet and said so. Fresh peas! How absolutely heavenly! And whole fresh strawberries, not mushy frozen berries spread thin in vanilla ice cream the way they were served at school. Mrs. MacLane smiled with pleasure at her daughter's praise.

When Barbara had cleared the dishes from the table, Mr. MacLane peeled the cellophane from his cigar, leaned back in his chair, and said, "Don't you think you should have stayed in Berkeley to study when you have mid-terms coming up?" he asked.

Rosemary rolled the edge of her place mat back and forth between her fingers. "I brought my books with me."

"Come on, Gordy, help me with the dishes," said Barbara hastily, although she longed to stay in the dining room. But Rosemary had a right to a little privacy in her own house. Anyway, if her father acted the way she thought he would, they would be able to hear every word he said in the kitchen. Gordy, somewhat to her surprise, actually followed Barbara into the kitchen, and he closed the swinging door behind him.

"I don't have to help with the dishes," Gordy said. "I just don't want to be around when Dad starts preaching to Rosemary about her grades. He might start in on me next."

"Oh, come on, Gordy," coaxed Barbara. "It won't hurt you for once. You can give the scraps to your cat." Buster was underfoot, as he always was when someone was in the kitchen.

While Barbara scraped the plates, Gordy presented a pea to Buster on the tip of his finger. He found a bit of meat also, and then to Barbara's surprise he actually picked up a dish towel. Gordy was so unpredictable. He could just as easily have gone into his room, shut the door, and started plinking on his guitar.

Barbara was torn between making a normal amount of noise in the kitchen and trying to be quiet enough to hear the conversation in the dining room. She was suddenly aware of a long silence on the other side of the swinging door. Then her mother said in such a sad voice, "Oh, Rosemary, you are so young," that it sent an unexpected pang through Barbara. It hurt to know her mother was sad.

Mr. MacLane did not sound sad at all as he said, "Married? At your age? Marriage isn't a date for a prom, you know."

Mrs. MacLane said, "I'm sure Greg must be a nice boy if you want to marry him, but we don't know a thing about his family."

Rosemary was trying to be patient. "I'm eighteen, Mother, and Greg is twenty-four. He isn't a boy. And I am not marrying his family. I am marrying Greg."

There was a snort from Mr. MacLane. "You may think you aren't marrying his family, but—"

Barbara had to start running the dishwater or have her family wonder why she was being so quiet. She turned the faucet on full force to fill the pan as quickly as possible. When she turned off the water she strained to hear.

"But Dad, we *love* each other," Rosemary was saying. "*That's* why we want to get married."

So the debate was on.

Gordy looked incredulous. "Did you hear that?" he asked hoarsely.

Barbara tried to wave him into silence with a soapy hand, but he was not to be silenced. "What does she want to go and get married for?" he asked in a whisper.

"You hear her," said Barbara.

"A-ah, love. That stuff," muttered Gordy, as he closely examined the saucers that had been cleared from the table. Those that looked clean he shelved in the cupboard.

"Gordy, you stop that." Barbara was even more impatient with her brother than usual. "You aren't supposed to put dishes back in the cupboard without washing them."

"Why not?" asked Gordy. "They look clean to me."

"Yes, but they have been handled," Barbara answered in a whisper, trying at the same time to catch what was being said in the dining room.

"But Dad, what do you have against Greg?" Rosemary was demanding to know.

"I don't have anything against Greg," said Mr. MacLane. "I think you are too young and too impractical for marriage."

"Yes, Rosemary," said Mrs. MacLane. "We have nothing against Greg. We just think you should wait until you are older."

"But I told you. Greg isn't eighteen," Rosemary was saying. "He's twenty-four, and he has his degree and is working for his teaching credential."

"And what about *your* education?" Mr. MacLane demanded.

Gordy dropped a handful of silverware on the floor, gathered it up, and returned it with a splash to Barbara's dishwater. Barbara glared at him.

"Well, I didn't do it on purpose," he said defensively.

The voices in the dining room were rising.

"But I *told* you. I am going back to school while he gets his general secondary credential. That's why we're going to summer school—so we won't have to carry so many courses next fall. Greg wants me to finish college. He believes women should use their minds."

"You're only making a C average now. How do you

think you'll manage when you have to keep house? Be practical for once in your life."

"I am being practical. Don't you see? We'll be settled then. It will be easier to study."

"Settled!" Mr. MacLane fairly snorted. "Keeping house in some two-room apartment. You call that settled?"

"Yes." Rosemary was stubborn.

"Well, I don't." Mr. MacLane was equally stubborn.

"Didn't Mother trail you around from one army camp to another when you were first married?" demanded Rosemary. "She didn't even have two rooms. I've heard her tell about the place in Texas where you had one room and shared a kitchen with eight other wives. Did you call that any way to start a marriage?"

That's a good point, thought Barbara. It must have been effective, because her father did not answer immediately.

"Boy," said Gordy. "They're sure going at it."

"Be quiet." Barbara rubbed a scouring pad around the inside of a pan to relieve her feelings. Her happy dream of a beautiful wedding for Rosemary was fading away. It was all so serious now. And that was right, of course. Marriage was serious. But couldn't they be serious and happy at the same time? Couldn't they agree about a few things? If only her mother did not sound so sad. And if only her father would stop raising his voice. Of course he was concerned about Rosemary's future, but he did not have to shout, did he? Barbara felt as if she could not bear it any longer. She wanted to weep into the dishwater, not only for her sister but for her mother and father, too.

"I told you Greg has a job," Rosemary was saying. "A perfectly good job in the Radiation Laboratory. He files things and looks up things at the library for the physicists, and he's good at it. The University raised his pay. We aren't going to starve."

"And can he afford to pay the the orthodontist twenty-five dollars a month?" Mr. MacLane demanded. "Have you thought of that little expense?"

"No . . . I haven't." Crestfallen, Rosemary faltered.

How awful, thought Barbara as she poured out the dishwater. To want to get married when you are still having your teeth straightened. It must be humiliating to have part of your childhood left over. And she could not help wondering if Greg could really afford to pay Rosemary's orthodontist. If she stopped wearing retainers now, her teeth might go crooked again, and she would have to start all over. That would be expensive. She was sure Greg could not afford it. Not and pay rent and buy groceries and a lot of other things Barbara had not thought about until now.

Mrs. MacLane came through the swinging door. Her face was flushed and she looked worried. "You children run along to the movies," she said. "You can take the money out of my purse, and Barbara, you can drive the car."

"I don't want to go to the movies," protested Gordy. "I'm working up a new arrangement for the trio."

"Come on, Gordy," said Barbara, distressed by her mother's flushed and anxious face.

"Yes," said Mrs. MacLane, leaving no doubt in her voice. Gordy was to go to the movies.

"O.K., Ma," said Gordy, and his mother was too preoccupied to tell her son not to call her Ma.

Barbara knew better than to protest that she did not want to go to the movies either. No girl wanted to be seen in public on Friday night with her younger brother, especially when that brother was wearing sneakers. She considered saying she would not go unless Gordy took off the sneakers and put on shoes, but in the interests of family peace she held her tongue. She would keep her eyes away from his feet and hope that everyone else did, too.

"And what about children?" Mr. MacLane was demanding as Barbara and Gordy were leaving the house. "Have you thought about them?"

"Of course we have thought about children," was Rosemary's heated answer.

"Whew!" said Gordy as he closed the back door.

"Whew is right," said Barbara, in rare agreement with her brother.

"I don't see why we have to be shoved out just because Dad and Rosemary are going at one another," said Gordy. "I don't see why old Rosemary has to go and get married anyway."

Barbara inserted the key in the ignition, a gesture that had been permitted her for only a few months. "Because she's in love, that's why. And you won't be losing a sister. You'll be gaining a brother-in-law." And so will I, she thought. A real live brother-in-law was a detail she had omitted from her dreams of a wedding in the family.

Gordy did not appear to be amused at her weak attempt at humor, and they rode in silence down the hill to the main street. Barbara felt embarrassed to be alone with Gordy, since they had quarreled so much lately, and she suspected her brother was experiencing much of the same feeling. Barbara searched for a diagonal parking space that she could slide into with ease, but found none. She turned a corner and found an empty space that unfortunately would require her to park parallel under Gordy's critical eye. Gordy, sensitive because he was the only member of the family too young for a driver's license, was inclined to make caustic remarks about Barbara's driving whenever he got a chance. Nervously Barbara pulled up beside the car parked ahead of the empty space. She put the car in reverse and started turning the wheel while she stepped lightly on the gas. The car moved faster than she had anticipated and banged the bumper of the one behind.

"That's right," said Gordy. "Take off a couple of fenders while you're at it."

"Oh, be quiet," snapped Barbara, as she shifted and tried again. She felt better, and her embarrassment at being alone with her brother was gone. Gordy was back to normal again.

Barbara and Gordy continued to feel shoved aside the rest of the weekend. When they returned from the movie, a gloomy Italian film neither had wanted to see, Mr. MacLane was sitting in the living room puffing on another cigar and staring at the cold ashes in the fireplace. Mrs. MacLane was nowhere in sight, and when Barbara went to her own room she found Rosemary, her face red and blotched from crying, sitting in front of the dressing table putting her hair up on rollers.

"Pretty awful?" Barbara asked softly.

Rosemary nodded. Two tears spilled from her red-rimmed eyes, slid down her cheeks, and plopped into a pile of bobby pins. She looked so miserable Barbara felt like crying herself. Rosemary wound a roller into a lock of hair as two more tears slid down her cheeks and into the bobby pins.

"If you keep that up, your bobby pins will rust," said Barbara with a shaky laugh.

Rosemary reached for a soggy wad of Kleenex and mopped her eyes.

"He . . . he didn't talk you out of it, did he?" ventured Barbara.

Rosemary shook her head.

"You could marry him anyway, no matter what Dad says," Barbara reminded her sister. "You are eighteen."

Rosemary looked at her own despairing face in the mirror and let out a quavering breath, half sob, half

sigh. "B-but I want everything to be h-happy," she
managed to say.

And so did Barbara. A wedding should be a time of
joy, and any tears that fell should not be the kind
Rosemary was shedding into her bobby pins. They
should be tears of happiness. Barbara prepared for
bed quickly. After she had turned out the light she
heard her mother and father talking long and earnestly in their room. A muffled sniff came from Rosemary's bed. Barbara began to dread the next day.

On Saturday the argument continued. Rosemary
said, Couldn't her father see? Times were so uncertain
that she and Greg wanted to get married before something terrible happened to the world. Mr. MacLane
wanted to know when in the history of the world had
times ever been certain. This argument took place at
breakfast. By lunch time the argument had swung
around to Mr. MacLane's saying, "And I suppose you
are going to tell me two can live as cheaply as one."

"Certainly not," was Rosemary's answer, "but two
can live as cheaply as two. Greg will be able to work
more hours by not taking as many courses. We have it
all figured out. The extra money he will earn will
equal the allowance I have been getting."

Please, Dad, thought Barbara, please, *please* don't
bring up Rosemary's orthodontist.

"Two married people cannot live as cheaply as two
single people," argued Mr. MacLane. "A married couple is equal to more than the sum of its parts. A couple needs to carry life insurance and hospital insurance. They need to think of the future in a way that
single people do not. They need pots and pans and
furniture—"

"But think of the saving in rent," interrupted Rosemary. "Oh, Dad, what's the use? You talk to Greg
when he comes over this evening. He'll tell you. He'll
make you understand."

Mrs. MacLane sent Gordy out to mow the lawn and told Barbara to go downtown and buy some thread and seam tape, so she could shorten Rosemary's coat.

"I'm coming with you," said Rosemary. And as soon as the girls were out of the house she said to Barbara, "Give me all your small change. I've got to phone Greg. I can't let him walk in tonight without any warning."

The girls stopped at a glass telephone booth in a service station. Rosemary stepped inside, closed the door, and put through her call, while Barbara watched the expressions that moved across her sister's face. Joy, briefly, when she heard Greg's voice, anxiety, earnestness, a tender smile, and, finally, calm. She emerged from the booth considerably more serene than she had entered it. "You know," she mused, "maybe Greg is right. He said probably most fathers acted this way when their first daughter got married. And he said not to worry. He will talk to Dad tonight. He will make him see our side."

"I hope he's right about fathers acting this way over the first wedding in the family," said Barbara. "I wouldn't want to go through this again when I get married." At the same time she thought, Poor Greg, wait till Dad gets hold of him.

"That's the way it has always been," said Rosemary. "I always have to argue about things with Dad first, and then you come along and want to do the same thing at the same age, and he doesn't even fuss. Remember how he acted when I first started wearing lipstick and bought my first pair of high heels? And two years later you did the same thing, and he didn't even seem to notice."

"You sound like a regular trail blazer," said Barbara. "Pocahontas leading Lewis and Clark."

"You mean Sacagawea."

"Well, some Indian."

This seemed to cheer Rosemary, but Barbara was not so sure that marriage was in the same class with lipstick and high heels. They bought the seam tape and thread in the dime store, and when they returned home, Rosemary went to her room and spent the rest of the afternoon studying. Barbara tried to settle down with some irregular French verbs, but she had trouble concentrating on them. She would think she was memorizing the tenses, only to discover that, in the back of her mind, she had been concentrating, not on a verb, but on Rosemary.

By dinnertime both Rosemary and her father seemed calmer, but neither one said much at the table. Mrs. MacLane looked weary and somehow older. The rice had a slightly scorched taste, but no one mentioned it. Only Gordy seemed really hungry. They all understood that Mrs. MacLane had not been able to put her mind on her cooking. Dessert was canned apricots and Girl Scout cookies, a further sign that Mrs. MacLane had no interest in food that evening.

After dinner Gordy, with an air of escaping, left the house with his guitar to practice with the other two members of his trio. Barbara wished she could escape, too, and wondered if she should have accepted Tootie's invitation to the movies. She was torn with a feeling, that was rapidly becoming familiar, of wanting to get away and of not wanting to miss anything. Not long after Gordy left, the doorbell rang, and the two sisters' eyes met in one tense, understanding look. "I guess I'll go study or something," said Barbara.

"Wait and say hello," whispered Rosemary, as she opened the door for Greg.

Barbara was surprised when Greg stepped into the room, because he looked older than she had remembered him and much more serious. There was an air of determination about him that she had not noticed before. She also observed that he had a fresh haircut, and she was touched by this. Poor Greg. That haircut told her that in spite of his seeming assurance, he was anxious, too. Rosemary straightened his tie, which really did not need straightening, in a wifely, possessive gesture.

"Hello, Barbara," he said, accepting Rosemary's gesture with a smile.

"Hello, Greg," answered Barbara, with a reticence she had not felt when she had thought of him as just another one of her sister's dates. "Well . . . I guess I had better go study."

In her room Barbara sat down cross-legged on her bed with her French verbs once more. She heard her mother and father greeting Greg, and for the second time that day her mind was not on her studying. She went over the present subjunctive and the imperfect subjunctive of *avoir*, only to have them slip right out of her mind without a trace. If Rosemary's affairs were not settled one way or another soon, she would probably flunk out of school, because she seemed incapable of learning anything anymore. She closed her book. This was a waste of time, but she had to find something to do as long as she was trapped in her room. She decided to paint her fingernails, something she rarely did anymore, because she considered the task tiresome and a waste of time.

Barbara opened Rosemary's drawer and found an assortment of bottles she had left behind when she went away to college. She examined the different shades and names and selected a bottle labeled "Chili Bean." From the living room came the sound of her father's voice speaking seriously. Barbara bit nervously at a hangnail, remembered she was supposed to be manicuring her nails, not biting them, and clipped the hangnail off with the nail scissors. Then she began to smooth her nails with an emery board in long, careful strokes. She had the whole evening before her and only ten fingers to work on.

The sound of voices from the living room was steady. Now Greg was speaking. Now Mr. MacLane. Neither raised his voice, which Barbara felt was a good sign. Never had nails been painted with such meticulous care. Each was filed to a perfect curve, each cuticle was pushed back until perfect half-moons showed. The Chili Bean polish was tried, rejected, removed with cotton and polish remover, and replaced with a different red. Still the voices murmured on, now Rosemary, now her mother, but most often Greg and Mr. MacLane.

Barbara's mouth felt dry. She wished she dared leave the bedroom to get a drink of water, but she did not want to risk interrupting the conversation at what might be a crucial moment. She finally settled on a third shade of polish, called "Tickled Pink," and began to paint her nails in careful strokes, sweeping from the half-moon to the tip. She worked slowly and carefully to pass the time. When all ten nails were painted she wafted her fingertips through the air to dry them. The voices continued.

Having nothing else to do, Barbara kicked off her slippers and went to work on her toenails with the same careful strokes she had used on her fingernails. This is a stupid way to spend an evening, she thought impatiently. No matter what Rosemary did, her life would go on, but once having started her toenails she felt she had to finish. When the job was completed she lay back on the bed and fanned her legs back and forth to dry the polish, wishing as she did so that she had been stricter with herself about concentrating on those unlearned French verbs, which now remained to spoil her Sunday.

A sudden burst of laughter from the living room made Barbara sit up, tense and listening. This was the first encouraging sign since Rosemary's telephone call last Tuesday. There was more conversation and another burst of laughter. What could be going on out there? She longed so much to know that she tiptoed across the room and pressed her ear to the door.

Then Rosemary's heels came clicking down the hall. Barbara skipped away from the door, sat down on the bed, and began innocently to fan her feet once more just as Rosemary burst into the room. Her pink cheeks and sparkling eyes told Barbara all she needed to know. Everything was fine. There was going to be a wedding, after all.

"Greg is going to drive me back to school tonight, so I can get more studying done tomorrow. Oh, I'm so happy I could *die*," whispered Rosemary, closing the door behind her.

"Oh, Rosemary!" Barbara was so happy for her sister she could find no words equal to the occasion and could only repeat, "Oh, Rosemary!"

"Greg was *marvelous* with Dad—very man to man and everything." Rosemary gathered her books together to take back to school. "He pointed out that he had his degree and could earn enough to support us both while he got his teaching credential and that I wouldn't have to work. And he said he wanted me to go on to school. I think that made a big impression on Dad—that Greg was really anxious for me to go on to school. But what really got him was when Greg said he wanted me to bring up my grades. That really won Dad over. And then Mom stepped in and said she was happy I had found someone as fine as Greg."

"What did Dad say then?" asked Barbara curiously, as Rosemary pulled her coat from the closet.

"He said he thought I was pretty young and he would rather we waited, but as long as our minds were made up, he guessed there was nothing he could say except to wish us happiness."

"Are you going to wash Greg's socks?" Barbara asked so suddenly she was surprised by her own question.

"How romantic! Is that all that interests you?" asked Rosemary with amusement. "I don't know. I never thought about it." As she slipped into her coat she appeared to be considering the matter. "Maybe I could buy him nylon socks, and when I rinsed out my nylons, he could rinse out his."

"I guess that takes care of Greg's socks," said Barbara with a giggle.

"I don't know. Maybe not. Maybe I'll wash them with loving care and stretch them on stretchers." Rosemary paused in front of the mirror to pull a comb through her hair. She was lovely to look at in her relief and her joy. She lingered a moment, struck by her own radiance. Then she turned her back to the mirror to face her sister. "There's just one thing that worries me," she said seriously.

"What?" asked Barbara, thinking of that monthly bill from the orthodontist.

"What on earth will I do about putting up my hair after I'm married?" asked Rosemary. And without waiting for an answer she was gone.

Chapter Four

The Monday morning after it was decided there was to be a wedding in the family, after all, Barbara and her mother were hurrying to change all the sheets in the house before they left for school. Barbara had removed her stuffed animals, had pulled the spread and blankets from her bed, and was about to remove the sheets when Buster came running down the hall to spring into the middle of the bed.

"You old pussycat," said Barbara. "Do you think I'm going to play change-the-sheet with you?" With Gordy out of the house she could speak to the cat with a sort of grudging affection as she folded the sheet over him and rolled him up in a loose bundle. Buster began to kick with his hind legs. Barbara poked at the bundle. Buster kicked back through the sheet. It was a game they played once a week.

"Don't you think that's a little hard on the sheets?" asked Mrs. MacLane, who was waiting, clean sheet in hand.

Barbara rolled Buster over inside the sheet. He poked out one black velvet paw and patted at her. "Yes, I guess it is," she agreed, "but Buster would be disappointed if we didn't play his game." She unrolled the sheet and dumped the cat on the floor, where he immediately began to wash his rumpled fur.

Barbara helped her mother unfold the clean sheet and spread it on the bed. They were alone in the house, and it seemed like a good moment for confidences. Barbara could contain her curiosity no longer. "Mother, what kind of a wedding do you think Rosemary will want?" she asked, as they spread the second sheet on top of the first.

"A simple one I hope." Mrs. MacLane leaned over to smooth out the wrinkles. "There's so little time to make plans. I do wish they would decide to wait until the end of summer session, so we would have a little more time, but their minds are made up. I guess we should be thankful she has settled on someone as fine as Greg."

"I know." Barbara knew her mother was thinking of some of the other boys Rosemary had liked. There was Jack, who couldn't graduate with his class in high school because he flunked English, but who had his own yellow convertible. What their father had had to say about him! And Roger, who was the handsomest boy in school and who combed his hair in front of a mirror every chance he got. "Mirror, mirror, on the wall. Who is the fairest of them all," Barbara had chanted whenever his name had come into the conversation, and the whole family always answered, "Roger!" Roger did not last long. Then there was Humphrey, who ran the eight-eighty in one minute, fifty-six seconds and who never treated Rosemary to Cokes or malts because he was in training. Old Fleetfoot the family called him. For several years boys had come and boys had gone, and Rosemary had gone steady with them all.

"This spread isn't even," said Mrs. MacLane. "You had better pull it over your way a few inches."

Barbara did as she was told and then began to arrange her stuffed animals. At sixteen she still loved the fat curve of Pooh Bear's stomach, and she hugged him before she laid him against her pillow. "But didn't Rosemary say a single word about the wedding?" she persisted, setting the stuffed penguin and the pink velvet pig beside him.

"Not a word. As soon as your father relented and wished them happiness, she and Greg left." Mrs. Mac-Lane bundled up the sheets that had been removed from the bed. "I hope she phones soon and gives us some clue to her plans. Six weeks is not a very long time for planning a wedding. And we must do something about Greg's family right away."

Barbara glanced out the window at the sky, saw that it was clear, pulled a sweater out of a drawer, gathered up her books, said good-by to her mother, and left the house without interrupting her train of thought. Rosemary was eighteen, Barbara was sixteen. That was a difference of only two years. Maybe two years from now. . . . Barbara, who had never had any very specific thought about her own marriage, began to wonder. Maybe at last she had found out what she wanted to do—get married in two years like Rosemary.

Two short years were not much over seven hundred days. Thinking in terms of days instead of years made Barbara feel as if she had not much time left. If she was going to get married in seven hundred days she should think about falling in love, and the sooner the better. Right now. Today. Until this minute she had thought of falling in love as something that would happen a long time from now. She had felt sorry for the girls she had known who had married right after graduation from high school. She even felt a little pity for a girl at school who was wearing a real engagement ring, because it was such a short step from a ring to a lifetime of dishwashing. Barbara, unlike some of the other girls, considered the engaged girl a poor old has-been, with nothing much left to live for. But now, recalling Rosemary's radiance and—to be perfectly honest—the attention she was going to get,

Barbara was beginning to change her attitude and to wonder if there was something she could do to speed up love. All she needed was a boy.

Tootie Bodger would not do. Definitely not. Of course Tootie would probably fill out and cheer up as he grew older, but Barbara did not want to wait that long. She wanted to fall in love now, in the springtime while the hills were green. She wanted to fall in love while Rosemary was having so much fun planning her wedding.

And so Barbara took particular care to avoid Tootie, lest he ask her for another date or she become known as Tootie's girl because she was seen with him around school. She ducked in one door of the library and out the other when she saw his head above the crowd in the hall. If she could go to class a roundabout way, she did so. Once she even ran up the staircase plainly labeled "Down only." She did succeed in avoiding Tootie, but the task was so time-consuming she could only smile and say hello to other boys as she scurried out of Tootie's path.

After a couple of days of this Barbara began to feel guilty about the way she was treating Tootie, who, after all, was really a very nice boy. She allowed him to catch up with her between classes one day when she knew they would have only a few minutes for talking. Then, anxious to prevent him from asking her to go to the movies again, she chattered so lightly and brightly about nothing at all that he did not have a chance to say anything and, looking puzzled and hurt, left her at the door of her classroom. Barbara felt guiltier than ever. She didn't *want* to hurt his feelings.

While Barbara dodged Tootie at school, at home she wondered with her mother about Rosemary's wedding plans. She and her mother tried to guess what sort of wedding she would want, and Barbara brought a book on wedding etiquette home from the library.

They took turns reading it and exclaiming over bits of information they had not known before. "Mother!" Barbara cried. "It says here that if the bride wants to wear a face veil, it can be held in place by a basting thread, and when it is time for her to remove it, her attendant *pulls the basting thread*. How perfectly ghastly. I know I could never find a basting thread in all that tulle."

"I never heard of such a thing," said Mrs. MacLane. "A face veil is usually just folded back over the bride's head. Anyway, I doubt if Rosemary chooses to wear one. And, of course, she may not choose you to be her maid of honor. She may want to ask Millie."

She wouldn't do that, thought Barbara, and began to speculate about the other attendants. Probably her roommate, Millie, who was a rather stolid, untidy girl. Barbara could not understand why Rosemary was fond of Millie. And perhaps Greg's sister Anne, the Physical Education major. And then there was their cousin Elinor, but perhaps she was too young. She was only twelve.

When Mrs. MacLane had a turn at the book, she read aloud menus for wedding receptions and despaired over the elaborate salads and sandwiches. She was the kind of cook whose gelatine salads would never come out of their molds without breaking. "Why doesn't Rosemary phone?" Mrs. MacLane asked several times a day. "We can't plan a thing until we at least know what time of day she wants the wedding. And I would like to know what she wants us to do about Greg's family." She hesitated to make the call herself, because Rosemary was not ready to have all the girls hear her discuss her wedding plans.

By Friday afternoon, as Barbara skipped out of the side entrance of the school building to avoid being walked home by Tootie, she felt that the whole week was a disappointment. She had not fallen in love, and the wedding had not been planned. What a waste of time. She decided to walk down Main Street instead of her usual street, because Tootie's legs were long and he could quickly catch up with her if she followed her usual route. Also, it had rained during the day, and since she had forgotten to bring a scarf for her hair, she could dodge under some of the awnings on Main Street.

And that was how it happened that Barbara was halted in a spring rain by one of Bayview's three traffic lights on a Friday afternoon on Main Street. A sound truck, blaring *Chattanooga Choochoo* in the center lane of traffic, forced Barbara's attention to turn toward the street. The sign on the truck carried a cartoon of a horse and the words, "Don't horse around. Call Joe's T.V. Repair today."

Between Barbara and the sound truck was a boy named Bill Cunningham, sitting on a motor scooter. Barbara, who knew him only slightly, could not help smiling at him, because he was riding under a large black cotton umbrella, its handle stuck down the back of his neck to free his hands for driving the Vespa.

"On track forty-nine at a quarter to nine," screeched the sound truck.

As Barbara stood in the rain smiling at Bill, he startled her by taking his right hand off the handlebar, holding it out to her, and saying dramatically above the noise of the truck, "Barbara! They are playing our song. Shall we dance?"

Barbara burst out laughing, it was all so crazy. The idea that she and Bill Cunningham had a song, particularly *Chattanooga Choochoo*, was ridiculous, because she barely knew him and had never danced with him at all. Not that she wouldn't want to if she ever got a chance. Bill was a very attractive boy, good-looking, intelligent, confident. The light changed from red to green, and the truck driver, pulling *Chattanooga Choochoo* after him, moved on down the street. Barbara and Bill did not.

"Hop on," said Bill. "I'll give you a ride home."

"Why not?" answered Barbara, and glanced down at the straight skirt she was wearing that day. This time it was her own, not a castoff of Rosemary's.

"You can ride sidesaddle," said Bill.

Still amused by the whole situation, Barbara stepped over the water in the gutter and ducked under the black umbrella. With her books clutched in one arm she perched on the narrow passenger's seat behind Bill.

"Hang on," directed Bill.

Barbara grasped the low handle in front of her. Just before the signal changed to red once more, Bill started the scooter putting across the intersection. It all happened that fast, in the interval of one green light.

Barbara squealed. Her perch was more precarious than she had expected, and she felt unbalanced riding sidesaddle with a load of books in one arm. The pavement flew beneath her in a wet black streak that made her dizzy.

Bill reached behind his back for her hand, which he grasped and pulled around in front of him so that her arm was encircling his waist. "Don't be bashful," he flung back over his shoulder. "That handle is too low to be any good."

Barbara felt embarrassed at having her arm around Bill's waist, but there was nothing she could do about it now except press her cheek against the umbrella handle at the back of his neck. Barbara MacLane, of all people, riding sidesaddle on a Vespa through the streets of Bayview—it was crazy and it was fun.

Bill swerved the Vespa around a corner. Barbara

tried to hold back a little scream. She was sure that she and her books were going to slide into the gutter. She clutched the front of Bill's jacket in her fist.

Now they were gaining on the sound truck. "On track forty-nine at a quarter to nine" . . . their song. Bill increased his speed and began to steer the scooter in curves, so that Barbara swayed back and forth.

"Bill! Stop!" she pleaded.

"Getting seasick?" he called over his shoulder.

"No. I just don't want to die young."

Bill straightened his course. "You're much too pretty for an early grave."

"Thanks," said Barbara to the back of Bill's neck. "That's big of you."

"You're welcome," answered Bill cheerfully.

Bill putted across the bridge over the stream that bisected the residential neighborhood of Bayview. He went past the park with its bandstand left over from another era, past the public library, onto Barbara's street, and up the hill, where he stopped in front of the MacLanes' house and tipped Barbara off his scooter onto the curb.

"Whew!" Barbara smiled at Bill with the rain falling gently on her face. She noticed that the front of his jacket was a whorl of wrinkles where her hand had clutched it.

Bill grinned at her from beneath his umbrella.

Stalling for time, Barbara said, "At least I'm still in one piece." She wished she could ask him to come into the house, but she knew her mother was not home. Neither could she stand in the rain trying to prolong the conversation. "Well, thanks for the ride," she said, because there was nothing else she could say.

"You're welcome." Bill grinned at her. "I don't suppose you have anything to eat in the house?"

Barbara thought quickly. She did not want to come right out and say that she was not allowed to ask a boy to come in unless one of her parents was home, but having unexpectedly landed a boy, so to speak, she did not want to let him get away. She glanced at the front steps, which were out of the direction of the rain and under the wide overhang of the roof. Fortunately they were dry. "Have a seat," she said, gesturing toward the steps. "I'll go in and see what I can find."

Bill pulled the umbrella out of his jacket and collapsed it, before he kicked the stand under his scooter and left it parked at the curb. He sat down on the top step with the ease of someone sitting on a chair in the living room. Apparently he expected no explanation for not being invited into the house.

Barbara ran around to the back door. In the kitchen she found Gordy eating tuna fish out of the can with Buster at his feet. "You know Mother doesn't like you to do that," she scolded. "She wants you to make a sandwich if you are going to eat tuna."

Gordy ignored this. "I didn't know you liked ham," he remarked, presenting Buster with a flake of tuna fish on the tip of his finger.

"Ham?" Barbara was flinging open cupboard doors in search of something, anything, to feed Bill before he got away.

"You just rode home with a cunning ham." Gordy laughed heartily at his own poor joke and scraped the bottom of the tuna-fish can with a spoon.

"If I couldn't make a better joke than that, I'd keep still."

Barbara had a feeling the nickname would stick. From now on Bill Cunningham would be known in the MacLane household as the Cunning Ham, just as Rosemary's Humphrey had been known as Old Fleetfoot. She found the cooky jar empty. Gordy again. The cooky jar was always empty. She found a half a bag of corn chips that Gordy had missed, or perhaps had not got to yet, and poured two glasses of milk,

which she set on a tray and carried out the front door.
Bill was still sitting on the step. She set the tray down
and sat beside it. "Have some corn chips and a glass
of milk," she said hospitably.

"Thanks," said Bill, and crunched into a handful of
corn chips.

"Isn't it funny?" remarked Barbara. "I was planning
to bake some cookies this afternoon." Now why did I
have to go and say a thing like that? she asked herself.
It was simply not true. She had not baked cookies
since her junior-high-school cooking class.

Bill looked interested. "You were?"

Now Barbara was stuck with her fib. "Yes. The
cooky jar is empty." This was certainly true. Since her
mother had gone back to teaching, it was almost always empty.

"My mother never bakes coookies," said Bill, and
Barbara thought he sounded as if he wished she did.

"Doesn't she like to bake?" asked Barbara.

"I don't know. Anyway, she doesn't have time. She
has this big career and everything. She's pretty tired
when she gets home." He reached for another handful
of corn chips.

Mrs. Cunningham's career was well-known in Bayview. She commuted to San Francisco, where she
wrote advertising copy for a chain of women's clothing stores. She was always the most fashionably
dressed commuter at the bus station, and her clothing
always looked brand-new, as if she had bought it only
the day before. This was in sharp contrast to the house-
wives of Bayview, who were seen about town in
comfortably baggy slacks on cold days and in cotton
blouses and skirts on warm days.

"We eat out a lot," continued Bill, "but the store
pays Mom so much she can't turn them down. Every
time she tries to quit they give her more money."

Barbara could not find anything to say to this. Her family almost never ate in restaurants, and although she knew her mother and father could always use more money, they seemed satisfied with their pay as teachers. Her mother, she knew, was teaching because teachers were needed and not because she wanted more money, although of course the extra income was welcome, especially since Rosemary was in college.

"Anyway, Mom bought me the Vespa," said Bill.

Barbara was a little shocked by this statement. In her family a gift came from both parents, no matter which one earned the money that paid for it.

"But it sure would be nice if she baked cookies once in a while," continued Bill, searching the bag for the last of the corn chips.

Barbara began to feel sorry for him. She pictured him going home hungry to a cold house. At least in winter it might be cold, if his mother turned the furnace off before she went to work, but that was not probable since she earned so much money. At this time of year, even though it was raining, the weather was not very cold. She tried, but it was almost impossible to feel completely sorry for a boy like Bill.

"Well, I won't keep you any longer." Bill rose and opened his big black umbrella.

Barbara did not want him to go so soon. "Oh, you weren't keeping me from anything."

"The cookies," Bill reminded her.

"Oh—yes," said Barbara hastily. She considered for a moment before she added, "Drop by for a handful sometime." She was satisfied that she had struck the right casual note. She did not want him to think she was trying to trap him with cookies for bait.

"Thank you, ma'am." Bill managed to bow with a flourish and hold his umbrella over his head at the same time. "This was a lot better than eating a bag of

French fries at the drugstore. See you soon." With that he stuck the umbrella handle down the back of his neck, mounted his Vespa, and was off down the hill with a wave and a backward grin.

Barbara watched the umbrella disappear around a bend in the road and, still smiling, she turned and walked into the house. Bill Cunningham. The last boy she had ever expected to notice her. She liked him. She really did. She liked him the way she liked the fizz in ginger ale and the cherry on a sundae. That was Bill Cunningham, and maybe this was the beginning of love. What fun it would be if someday they could look back and say, "We fell in love—plunk, just like that—while a stop light changed from red to green."

Barbara considered Bill and wondered what her father thought of him. There was one good thing—Bill's name usually appeared on the honor roll—and, considering her father's attitude toward grades, anyone's grades, Barbara felt this was a real bonanza. She could not think of a single thing about Bill that her father could object to. He was a good student, he took part in school activities—but not to the extent that he could be called a big activity man—he was lively and full of fun, but he never got into trouble. He was, to use a phrase Rosemary used a lot since she went away to college, well-adjusted. There was, however, his Vespa to think about. Barbara wondered how her parents would feel about her riding around town on a motor scooter, but she quickly dismissed this small worry. If Rosemary had permission to get married, surely she could have permission to ride on a Vespa.

Barbara went into the house and took a quick inventory of the kitchen cupboards for cooky ingredients. There were no nuts or raisins, which eliminated a lot of recipes right there.

"I had an old dog. His name was Blue," sang Gordy from his room.

Barbara began to read cooky recipes. Brownies were out. She had no nuts. Checkerboard cookies. Too difficult. Refrigerator cookies. She did not want to wait for the dough to chill. Oatmeal cookies. Well . . . maybe. They weren't really good without raisins. Snickerdoodles. She liked the name. Sugar, flour, shortening, egg . . . roll into the size of a walnut . . . dip in sugar and cinnamon. They sounded good, and the recipe made four dozen. Gordy would probably smell the cinnamon while they were baking and demand some, but she should be able to hide most of them. . . .

Barbara got out a mixing bowl and measuring cup, but before she set about baking snickerdoodles for Bill Cunningham, she added raisins and walnuts to the shopping list on the cupboard door. "I'm falling in love," she whispered experimentally to herself, and found the words comfortable on her tongue.

Chapter Five

The next evening, while Mrs. MacLane and Barbara lingered at the table and Mr. McLane was enjoying his after-dinner cigar, Mrs. MacLane asked, "What are we going to do about Greg's family? We can't put it off any longer."

Barbara knew at least some of the answers, because she had skimmed through the book about weddings from the library. "The wedding books says the groom's family calls on the bride's family," she informed her mother.

"I know," said Mrs. MacLane, "but if they are going to drive fifty miles to call, it seems as if we should offer them a meal. And if we are going to do that, I think we should simply ask them to come for supper in the first place." No one had anything to say to this suggestion, so she continued. "I wonder what the Aldredges are like."

"Rosemary says Greg's father has made a lot of money in the luggage business," volunteered Barbara, "but he's not terribly intellectual."

Her father scowled through a cloud of cigar smoke. "And since when did I raise my daughter to be a snob?" he asked.

"Now what on earth did Rosemary mean by a remark like that?" demanded Mrs. MacLane.

"Oh . . . you know . . ." said Barbara vaguely.

"He doesn't go to museums and concerts and things like that."

"And neither did Rosemary until she went away to college," Mrs. MacLane pointed out. "And if that is her definition of culture, I'm afraid your father and I don't measure up either. At least not for a long time. Not since we had three children.

"He's probably been too busy earning money, so he could educate his family," said Mr. MacLane, leaning back in his chair once more. "The poor fellow probably hasn't had time to do anything else, with three children in college. Too busy keeping his nose to the grindstone."

"Greg has supported himself since he went into the Air Force," Barbara informed her father.

"Well, don't keep us in suspense. Tell us all," said Mrs. MacLane. "What did Rosemary say about Greg's mother?"

"Oh, she's all right, I guess," said Barbara. "Anyway, Rosemary says Greg doesn't let her bother him anymore. He's very mature about it. She used to bother him until he went into the Air Force, but he's past that stage now. He says she's a nice gal." Barbara was not prepared for her parents' reaction to this bit of information.

"Well!" said her mother.

"I'll be darned," said her father.

Barbara was anxious to make her parents understand. "But Rosemary says it's important to rebel against your parents. Otherwise, nobody ever grows up."

"Oh, she does, does she?" Mr. MacLane knocked the ash off his cigar into the ash tray Barbara had fetched when dessert was finished.

"I suppose in a way she's right," reflected Mrs. MacLane, "but somehow I don't like her to be so blunt about it."

"It seems to me," said Mr. MacLane, "that ever since Rosemary has been going to the University she has been talking like someone who has read a book on psychology."

"I don't know why," puzzled Mrs. MacLane. "She isn't even taking psychology."

Barbara had the explanation. "But her roommate is. Millie is majoring in psychology. Rosemary learns a lot from her."

"How nice," said Mrs. MacLane dryly. "I am so glad we are to share in the benefits of Millie's college education."

Mr. MacLane exhaled a large blue cloud of smoke. "Well, let me tell you something. Someday some mother is going to rebel against her children, and when she does, I will be the first to contribute to a statue in her honor, to be placed downtown in the center of the plaza. A bronze statue. And each year on Mother's Day I shall personally lay a wreath at her feet."

"Oh, Dad." Barbara's tone implied, Don't be silly. "Rosemary says—"

Mrs. MacLane interrupted. Apparently she did not want to hear any more of what Rosemary had to say. "At least we know Greg's mother is a nice gal. Or so Greg says. Shall we ask the Aldredges for Sunday-night supper or shall we not? If we do we had better have them soon, because June is coming closer every day."

"Sure," agreed Mr. MacLane expansively. "The old man and I ought to get along just fine. We can talk about baseball and other nonintellectual subjects."

"Dad, please don't make a big thing out of what Greg said." Barbara was impatient, more with herself than with her father. Knowing her father's talent for worrying a subject the way a dog worries a bone, she never should have repeated verbatim what Rosemary had confided, but somehow the remarks about Greg's parents had sounded different when Rosemary had made them. Barbara had been impressed by Rosemary's and Greg's adult, detached attitude. They had seemed so emancipated, so mature. But now she was no longer certain. Maybe they were just disloyal.

"Who's making a big thing of it?" Mr. MacLane asked in his jovial after-dinner manner. "You said Rosemary said Greg's father wasn't terribly intellectual. Well, neither am I. And, I might add, neither is Rosemary."

"Oh, Dad. You are, too, making a big thing out of it," Barbara informed him. "I'm sorry I ever mentioned it. Just forget all about it." But she knew her father would not. This was too good a topic for his talent for banter.

There was a slight frown mark between Mrs. MacLane's eyebrows. "What do you suppose Greg has told his family about us?" she wondered aloud. "He really doesn't know us very well, and there's no telling what he may think or what Rosemary may have told him."

"She probably says her father is a little crude, but a good egg," suggested Mr. MacLane. "And she probably says condescendingly that you are a good kid who doesn't use her mind." Mr. MacLane had never let Rosemary forget that she had once said the trouble with the members of her mother's club was they did not use their minds.

"I can't believe she'd say a thing like that," said Mrs. MacLane.

"Why not?" her husband wanted to know. "Kids nowadays feel they can say anything about their parents. This makes them well-adjusted, as Rosemary would probably say."

"For one thing, now that I have gone back to teaching, I think she has finally conceded that I do use my mind," said Mrs. MacLane.

What about me? Barbara began to wonder. What had Rosemary told Greg about his future sister-in-law? She rummaged through Rosemary's secondhand psychology jargon for phrases that might fit. Something like, "Barbara's all right but she's terribly immature." Or, "Barbara's all right but she can't get along with Gordy. Sibling rivalry, you know. She feels insecure." Then Greg would pass this along to his family, who would arrive expecting a very young girl quarreling with her brother. Barbara resolved to stop quarreling with Gordy at once. When the Aldredges arrived, she would be so poised and so grown-up that they would leave, asking one another, "Was that the girl Greg said was immature? Impossible! She and her brother got along beautifully." Yes, Barbara was going to have to watch her step.

That same evening Mrs. MacLane composed half a dozen drafts of a gracious note to Greg's mother and father, inviting them to come for supper Sunday evening. She read all versions aloud to Mr. MacLane, and when they agreed on the wording, the letter was written and mailed. Two days later an equally gracious note arrived accepting the invitation.

The acceptance precipitated a flurry of house cleaning and silver polishing. "This is supposed to be a friendly visit, not an inspection," Mr. MacLane reminded his wife.

Mrs. MacLane laid down the dustcloth and sighed. "I know, but I can't keep things looking the way they should when I'm teaching."

Barbara thought guiltily of the fluff of dust she had shoved back under her bed with her toe, and went to get the dust mop.

By late Sunday afternoon the house was shining,

Gordy had been persuaded into his gray suit, the table was set, and the salad greens were chilling in a plastic bag in the refrigerator. The family was ready for what Mr. MacLane persisted in referring to as the big powwow.

"Dad, please take off that green eyeshade," pleaded Barbara, trying to see the house and her parents through Rosemary's eyes. "You know Rosemary doesn't like you to wear it when her friends come here."

"They will have to take me as I am," said her father, but he removed the eyeshade and tossed it into his rolltop desk on the sunporch. When he was not looking, Barbara closed the top of the desk.

At six-thirty the doorbell rang, and Mrs. MacLane went to answer it. "Mr. and Mrs. Aldredge!" she exclaimed. "I'm so happy to meet you at last. We've been hearing so much about you."

We certainly have, thought Barbara, looking over the parents of the groom while trying not to appear as if she were inspecting them. The father was a ruddy, tweedy man, who was exchanging a hearty handshake with Mr. MacLane. Lots of golf, Barbara decided, and maybe hunting and fishing, too. He did not look like a man whose nose was worn down by a grindstone to keep his children in college. She turned her attention to Greg's mother, who was wearing a mink stole and a splashy silk print that only a very slim woman could wear. Barbara mentally summed her up as a pointed person—pointed features, pointed shoes, pointed fingernails. Barbara felt disloyal even thinking it, but Greg's mother made her own mother look plump and a little dowdy.

"We think a lot of Greg," Mrs. MacLane was saying. "He's a fine boy."

"Yes, a fine boy," echoed Mr. MacLane. "A boy to be proud of."

"And Rosemary is a darling girl," said the mother of the groom. "We couldn't be happier. The first time I met her I knew that this was the girl who was going to be my daughter-in-law."

When the mink stole was laid on the bed and the two families were seated in the living room, there was a sudden silence that both mothers rushed to fill.

"Greg says—" began Mrs. Aldredge.

"Rosemary says—" began Mrs. MacLane. Both women stopped and laughed.

Mr. MacLane felt this conversation needed masculine guidance. He turned to Greg's father and said, "I hear you are a baseball fan. How do you think the Giants will finish this year?"

Barbara darted a suspicious glance at her father. She thought from the remark he had made when this evening was being planned that perhaps he was trying to be funny, but apparently he was not. He was only following a well-known masculine axiom: When in doubt, bring up baseball. The two mothers exchanged sympathetic smiles.

"The odds are that they will finish second behind the Dodgers," said Mr. Aldredge, settling comfortably back in his chair as if he and Mr. MacLane discussed baseball every night of the week, "but it seems to me that with the pitchers they've got and the stronger bench, they should finish either first or second."

Mrs. MacLane excused herself to look at something in the oven. Barbara caught Mrs. Aldredge's glance sliding from the end of the sofa, which Buster had clawed to a woolly fringe, to the carpet, and then to the lamp shades. It was a shrewd glance, as if she was assigning price tags to everything in the room. I don't think I like her, Barbara thought suddenly.

"I'm not so sure about that," Mr. MacLane was saying. "I think the Dogers are a stronger all-around club, and if the hitters come through they'll take it."

Barbara felt that she was being immature. She should be making conversation with Greg's mother, who must have felt that she should be talking to the sister of the bride, because she smiled at Barbara and said, "You certainly look like Rosemary. I would have known you as her sister anywhere."

Striving to look poised and mature, Barbara returned the smile. It was always so hard to know what to say to this commonplace remark that everyone made. Her impulse was to say, Yes, but my hair is naturally curly. She dismissed this remark as lacking in maturity, and answered lamely, "I guess we do look quite a bit alike." She wished her mother would return to steer the conversation where it belonged—on the wedding.

Mr. Aldredge was saying, "I think the two new pitchers will mean eight to ten more wins, and the manager isn't experimenting with positions the way he did last year."

The wedding, thought Barbara, you are here to talk about the wedding. Then she had an inspiration. "Do Greg and his brother look alike?" she asked Mrs. Aldredge, hoping she sounded both mature and secure.

"Quite a bit," answered the mother of the groom. "Bob is taller. It used to bother Greg when the boys were younger. He didn't like being shorter than his younger brother."

Barbara was pleased with this bit of information about the brother, who was sure to be the best man. She liked tall boys, as long as they were not as tall as Tootie Bodger.

"Well, don't forget the wind is going to favor the home team, and that will mean another five to eight games," Greg's father was saying, and Barbara knew that once the men started talking about the wind at Candlestick Park, they were good for another half hour. They would have to discuss how the ball park should never have been built where it was in the first place and all the possibilities for remodeling it. It was a conversation she had heard many times and did not want to hear again at this particular moment.

"If you will excuse me, I think I had better help my mother," Barbara said to Mrs. Aldredge.

"Is there anything I can do to help?" Mrs. Aldredge asked.

"No, thank you," answered Barbara.

As she left the room Mrs. Aldredge was saying, "Now Ed, don't you think—"

"Mother," whispered Barbara in the kitchen, "*why* did you let Dad get started on baseball? They're here to talk about the wedding."

"They're here to get acquainted, and baseball is as good a subject as any. At least the men have that much in common." She lifted a lid, salted something in a saucepan, and then fanned her flushed face with a pot holder. "Empty the salad greens out of the plastic bag, will you, dear? The dressing is in the refrigerator."

When the meal was served, Gordy was produced and the two families seated. Much to Gordy's annoyance, Mrs. Aldredge admired his red hair, which he did not like and had once threatened to dye. The conversation swung around to the occupations of the men, and Barbara waited patiently while Mr. Aldredge told how he had come out to California and had bought a luggage shop. The shop had been so profitable that he was able to expand, and now he owned shops in several towns. That takes care of Mr. Aldredge, she thought when he had finished. Now for the wedding.

But no. It was Mr. MacLane's turn. He told how he had worked his way through college in a print shop where "we used to hand set legals in six-point solid, thirteen picas wide." Barbara knew this meant nothing to the Aldredges, but they were smiling gamely as if they understood everything her father was talking about. This brought her father to his favorite subject and one that he was proud of—how he had built up the high-school print shop from an old-time proof press, until his students were able to handle the yearbook and all the printing for the school district. Many of the printers in the area had been his students at one time. "And now most of those kids are earning more than I do," he concluded with pride.

Barbara forgot her impatience for a moment in her admiration for her father, who had helped a lot of boys who did not like school get a start in the world. Maybe he was a little exasperating around the house, but she loved him and she was proud of him. She sat at the table reminiscing about one of her childhood visits to her father's print shop, when he had given her a slug, hot from the Linotype machine, with her name spelled backward. To this day she loved the smell of printer's ink. At the moment this thought was passing through Barbara's mind, she caught the merest flicker of a glance pass between Mrs. Aldredge and her husband. She wondered what it meant. Were they confirming something Greg had told them about her father? Something like, "He's all right, but he does go on about that print shop of his." Or perhaps they were impatient because her father had talked too long, when they were eager to get on with a discussion of the wedding.

Apparently so. "Won't Rosemary make a lovely bride?" remarked Mrs. Aldredge, after Barbara had cleared away the plates and had served the dessert.

This was a difficult question for the mother of the bride to answer without sounding smug. Mrs. MacLane managed nicely. "Rosemary and Greg will make a very attractive couple," she said.

"That is just what I was telling Ed on the way over here," said Mrs. Aldredge. "I said, 'Ed, Rosemary and Greg will make one of the most attractive couples we have ever seen walk out of a church together.'"

And his brother and I will make an attractive best man and maid of honor, thought Barbara, eager to be part of the picture. The talk was desultory. Young people were so courageous these days to marry and continue their schooling. The Aldredges were willing to help Greg and Rosemary, but they refused to be helped. With such a strenuous program ahead of them, they would have to find an apartment close to the campus. The conversation was pleasant enough, but Barbara felt that the Aldredges were postponing something, that the real issue of the powwow was yet to come.

Mr. MacLane produced a cigar and extended it to Mr. Aldredge. "Care for a smoke?" he asked.

"Don't mind if I do," answered the father of the groom, accepting the cigar.

Barbara recognized her cue. She fetched the ash trays without being asked.

"Has Rosemary said anything about her plans for the wedding?" inquired Mrs. Aldredge, as the two men settled back to enjoy their cigars and Mrs. Mac-Lane served the coffee.

Mrs. MacLane smiled apologetically. "I'm afraid she hasn't. It has all happened so suddenly, and I know she's busy studying for mid-terms, so I've hesitated to telephone her. But she'll be home next weekend, and I'm sure we can begin planning then. Of course it's entirely up to Rosemary, but I thought a simple wedding, simple but pretty, you know—"

That's what I want when I get married, thought Barbara, and instantly Bill Cunningham, riding down the hill under his black umbrella, came to mind.

"Of course it is entirely up to Rosemary," agreed Mrs. Aldredge. "Now where did I leave my bag?"

"I'll get it for you," offered Barbara, even though she did not want to leave the table.

"Thank you, dear." Mrs. Aldredge smiled. Her magenta lipstick exactly matched the print in her dress.

Barbara went into her parents' room, where she was horrified to find Buster snoozing luxuriously on Mrs. Aldredge's mink stole. He was not only an elegant-looking cat, he had a taste for elegance as well. "Oh, you—" She snatched him up rudely with one hand and picked up Mrs. Aldredge's large patent-leather bag with the other. She went back to the dining room by way of the kitchen, where she dumped Buster, who was uttering Siamese oaths, out the back door. She handed Mrs. Aldredge her bag and glared at Gordy.

Her brother returned her look. "What did I ever do to you?" he demanded.

"Oh, that cat of yours," she answered impatiently. Then she thought, Oh dear, I mustn't talk this way. The Aldredges are probably thinking, Rosemary is right. Barbara can't seem to get along with her brother. Barbara managed to smile at Gordy. "It's nothing, really. Forget it." She glanced at Mrs. Aldredge, who was taking something out of her bag and apparently had not noticed that the siblings had narrowly avoided public rivalry.

"Gordy, you may be excused," said Mrs. MacLane, and Gordy, eager to get out of his white shirt and tie, left the table.

Mrs. Aldredge produced a pack of white cards and used them to fan away the cigar smoke before she smiled and said briskly, "I've already made a list of our friends and relatives who will expect to be invited to the wedding. I have them all listed in alphabetical order on cards, to make it easier for Rosemary. I have put a check in the corner of the card if the person can

actually be expected to come to the wedding. You will
need to have some idea what to tell the caterer."

The MacLanes stared at the stack of cards. There
were over a hundred, perhaps closer to two hundred.
Barbara could see that the names and addresses were
neatly typed, and although she was as dismayed as
she knew her mother must be at the size of the list
and the mention of a caterer, she could not help admiring Mrs. Aldredge's efficiency.

"Well. . . ." Mrs. MacLane seemed uncertain as to
what she should say. "Rosemary hasn't actually said
so, but I am quite certain she is planning a . . .
modest wedding."

Mrs. Aldredge dismissed this by saying, "Every girl
dreams of a big wedding." She fanned through the
cards with her pointed fingers. "And for years I have
been keeping a list of all the presents we have had to
buy for the children's friends—graduations, weddings,
showers—you know. And then there are all our relatives, although most of them live in the East and can't
be expected to come. And some of our closest business
friends. They will all be expecting invitations. Presents have cost us hundreds of dollars, and Rosemary
and Greg might as well get some of it back."

Barbara wondered uneasily what her father would
have to say about this eye-for-an-eye, tooth-for-a-tooth
philosophy of wedding invitations. He was sure to say
something, and she hoped that, whatever it was, it
would not cause Rosemary to have mother-in-law
trouble the rest of her life.

Mr. MacLane blew a puff of smoke toward the ceiling before he said, "Casting your bread upon the wa-
ters, eh?"

"In a way," agreed Mrs. Aldredge, missing the barb
of the remark.

Mr. Aldredge was more astute. "Now we don't want
you to ask more people than you feel you can—

handle." He had almost said "afford." "Maybe we could go through the list and mark those that are most important."

"But Ed," said Mrs. Aldredge, "Greg is our oldest child."

"Yes, but I told you on the way over here—"

"But Ed—"

The MacLanes exchanged uneasy glances, before Mrs. MacLane leaned forward and said, "I think we should talk it over with Rosemary. After all, we can't make any decisions until we know what she wants to do. I'm sure we can settle a lot of things this weekend, and if she really wants a big wedding, we can manage somehow."

"Of course we should talk it over with the bride," agreed Mrs. Aldredge graciously. She hesitated a moment before she said, "Please don't worry about the expense. Ed and I will be more than glad to help pay for the wedding."

Barbara felt shocked and humiliated. This must have been the meaning of the glance the Aldredges exchanged when her father had said many of his former students now earned more money than he did. This was why Mrs. Aldredge had cast an appraising look around the living room. The Aldredges thought the MacLanes could not afford to give Rosemary a nice-enough wedding for their friends to attend. They had talked it over on their way to Bayview and had agreed they should offer to help pay for it. Barbara's hurt quickly turned to anger at Greg's mother, sitting there at the dinner table, smiling her magenta smile. She did not like her, not one little bit. She did not like her pointed fingernails and pointed toes or her pointed looks and remarks, either.

Mrs. MacLane, whose face was flushed a becoming pink, said nothing. She was leaving the answer to this proposal to her husband. He took his time about answering. He sipped his coffee and flicked the ash off his cigar before he looked directly at Mrs. Aldredge and said, "No, thank you. That won't be necessary. We will give Rosemary the wedding she wants." He spoke pleasantly, almost quietly, but somehow everyone in the room knew there was nothing more to be said on the subject.

After that the two families left the table and exchanged small talk for a short time in the living room until the Aldredges began to mention the long drive home, the heavy Sunday-night traffic, work the next day. "Please don't think we are eating and running, but—"

"Dad!" exploded Barbara, when Greg's parents had gone. "Why didn't you tell her off? How could you just sit there and be so calm about it all? That woman insulted us!"

"What did you expect me to do?" asked her father. "Challenge her to a duel?"

Barbara smiled ruefully, realizing her father could not very well open a feud between the two families. That really would spoil the wedding. "Not a duel exactly, but maybe a polite fight," she said.

"I think your father got his point across," said her mother. "There was no need to say more."

"I figured it this way," said Mr. MacLane. "If Greg doesn't let his mother bother him, why should I? After all, I want to be mature, too."

Even now her father could joke, now when the family honor had been insulted. "I can't stand her," stormed Barbara, "and I feel sorry for Rosemary, having her for a mother-in-law all her life."

"I'm sure she meant well, even though her offer seems tactless to us," said Mrs. MacLane. "And I think we should try to remember that she is Greg's mother and that she had a lot to do with bringing him up to be the person he is."

"I suppose so," said Barbara grudgingly. It seemed to her that now a big wedding was necessary to save the honor of the MacLanes. I don't care if I am being immature and insecure, she thought, and wondered how Rosemary was going to feel about her future mother-in-law's offer.

Chapter Six

The next Saturday morning Rosemary, who had not asked Barbara to meet her at the bus station, arrived home immediately after her appointment with the orthodontist. Barbara, seeing that she was carrying only two books, knew at once that she was not planning to stay long, and was disappointed. She had counted on getting her sister alone to talk about Bill Cunningham, who had given her several rides home on his Vespa and had stopped for cookies and milk. She and Bill, with unwelcome help from Gordy, had eaten their way through a batch of snickerdoodles and were well into a batch of brownies. She felt she had to talk about Bill to someone, or she would fizz over like a bottle of ginger ale that had been shaken.

"Guess what?" Rosemary burst out as soon as she stepped through the door. "I got the dentist to admit that he'll take the bands off my teeth before the wedding!"

"For keeps?" asked Barbara.

"For keeps," answered Rosemary. "No more grillwork, no more trips to the orthodontist, no more monthly bills!"

"I'm glad to hear it." Mrs. MacLane laid down the coat she was at last finding time to shorten and said, "Rosemary, be sure to phone Aunt Josie and Gramma and tell them about the wedding. They'll be hurt if they aren't the first to hear it." Aunt Josie was Miss

Pennell, Mrs. MacLane's older sister. She lived with her mother, Mrs. Pennell, whom the MacLanes called Gramma.

"And what about Uncle Charlie?" asked Barbara.

"Yes, you should tell your Uncle Charlie, too," said Mrs. MacLane, "but your Aunt Josie and Gramma should be the first to know."

"Mother, promise you won't let Uncle Charlie try to sell Greg an insurance policy the very first thing," begged Rosemary.

Mrs. MacLane smiled. "I can't be responsible for your relatives. Now run along and phone Aunt Josie and Gramma."

"But, Mother, I have to study and you know how Aunt Josie is," protested Rosemary. "Besides, I have to go back to school right after lunch."

"Yes, I do know Aunt Josie," said Mrs. MacLane. "That's why I want you to tell her yourself."

I am not going to have a chance to get in one word about Bill Cunningham, not even edgeways, thought Barbara suddenly. This whole morning was going to belong to Rosemary. She was nothing but the sister of the bride.

"Have you thought about the wedding?" Mrs. Mac-Lane asked her older daughter.

"Sort of." Rosemary looked vague, happy, and unusually pretty. "Not much. Last week I was too busy thinking about what Dad was going to say, and this week I had to write a paper for English on *Love's Labour's Lost.*"

"Next month is June," Mrs. MacLane reminded her, bringing the conversation back to the wedding. "Hand me that seam tape, will you, dear?"

"I know." Rosemary was trying to look thoughtful. "I thought I'd be married in a suit. And a hat with a little veil."

A suit! Barbara did not have to hide her disappointment, because no one was paying the slightest attention to her. A suit would spoil everything. Being married in a suit might be legal and binding and all that, but it certainly would not be a wedding. And as for Mrs. Aldredge—she would probably be ashamed to invite her friends to such an affair. No, a suit would not do. Rosemary's mind would have to be changed. That was all there was to it.

Mrs. MacLane tore the cellophane from the seam tape. "How many guests are you planning to have?" she asked. "We have to start someplace."

"Just our families and maybe our roommates. I don't know." Rosemary's manner was offhand.

This was not the way to plan a wedding, thought Barbara. A wedding should have lots of guests, a whole churchful, in their best clothes. Gloves, flowered hats, everything. She could see her mother was about to say something but was choosing her words with care. There were so many things Barbara wanted to know that she could hold back no longer, and she seized the moment of her mother's hesitation. "When do you get your engagement ring?" she asked.

Rosemary smiled at her sister, but it was a new kind of smile, a smile one might bestow on a lovable and amusing child. "I'm not going to have an engagement ring. Just a plain gold band for the ceremony. We have so many more worthwhile uses for our money— tuition, for instance—and, anyway, engagement rings are so sort of, I don't know, middle-class." They were not even married yet, and already it was *their* money.

Barbara and her mother exchanged a glance at this astonishing statement. Mrs. MacLane, who wore a modest engagement ring, raised one eyebrow and said, "It is certainly news to me that engagement rings are middle-class."

"Oh, Mother, you know what I mean," said Rosemary vaguely.

"I'm afraid I don't." Mrs. MacLane's tone was tart, but she continued on a gentler note. "We want you to have the kind of wedding you want. But don't you think it would be a happier occasion if you were married in a pretty dress instead of a suit? If it's the money you're worried about, don't worry. We can manage a nice little wedding. Something simple but pretty."

Barbara was eager to encourage her sister for the sake of the family honor. "And Greg's mother thinks you should have a real wedding. She says, in her heart, every girl wants a big wedding."

"I don't," said the bride. "And Greg wants us to have whatever I want, and I am not going to have a big wedding just to impress his mother's friends. My family is giving the wedding, not his."

As much as she longed for a big wedding, Barbara could not help admiring her sister for the stand she was taking. Rosemary had grown up in the past year. She was no longer the kind of girl who would choose a dress simply because it bore a good label.

"But a suit seems a little severe," said Mrs. MacLane mildly.

"Oh, Mother, a wedding with bridesmaids and everything would be an awful bother. I'm just trying to be practical," said Rosemary. "You know how Dad is always saying how impractical I am. Well, this time I'm being practical. That's all."

Well, wouldn't you know! thought Barbara, as her dream of a lovely wedding faded like a bruised gardenia. *Now* Rosemary had to start being practical, after a whole life of being impractical. Next she would probably say she wanted pots and pans for wedding presents. Or a vacuum cleaner. Or a pail and scrubbing brush. If Rosemary decided to be practical, she would be all-out, one-hundred-per-cent practical. Rosemary, according to her father, always overdid things. In this mood she would probably decide to be married in a tweed suit, which would wear forever and grow baggy with age. "The bride, attired in sturdy Harris tweed of a sensible shade of brown, was given in marriage by her father," the papers would say, "and was attended by her sister, in gray tweed, with a bouquet of geraniums picked in the back yard." Or Rosemary would probably dismiss the thought of any attendants at all as being impractical.

"But a wedding should be an event to remember," protested Mrs. MacLane. "It is not a time for being practical."

"Of course it isn't," Barbara agreed, pleased with her mother, who, she now felt, was showing an unexpected streak of poetry in her soul.

Rosemary flashed her mother and sister an amused smile. "Honestly, Mother, I can't see why everybody always has to get so sentimental, just because two people decide to get married."

Now it was Mrs. MacLane's turn to look amused. "A wedding *is* an occasion for sentiment, and that's the way it should be. You can't escape sentiment, so why not have a pretty wedding?"

"Besides, think of the presents," said Barbara, as long as Rosemary was bent on being practical.

"Oh, presents." Rosemary dismissed wedding gifts with that irritating air of sophistication she had sometimes assumed since she had gone away to college. "They are mostly just *things*. Greg and I want a life free of *things*."

"Now what on earth do you mean by a remark like that?" Mrs. MacLane's exasperation was rising to the surface once more.

"I mean that if we have our lives cluttered up with a lot of *things*, I'll have to waste my time dusting them and taking care of them when I could be doing something more constructive. Except for books and records, we want a life free of possessions," explained Rosemary.

Barbara considered this with interest. She thought of her own half of their room cluttered with *things,* stuffed animals, a poster advertising a school play, faded pompons, and party invitations. Rosemary was right. Tomorrow she would clear out a lot of *things,* so her mother wouldn't spend so much time telling her to straighten up her room. At the same time she was upset at the idea of a wedding with no presents. Opening packages would be half the fun.

"That is all very well, dear," Mrs. MacLane said to Rosemary, as she pinned the tape to the edge of the coat, "but there is such a thing as being too practical. Your father and I couldn't have a wedding during the war, and although I didn't really mind, I'm sure your father wished things might have been different. It was all so bleak. The army camp had just been built, and it was nothing but a chapel and a PX and a lot of barracks in a sea of mud. Not a tree or a shrub anywhere. And your father about to go overseas."

Both girls looked with surprise and curiosity at their mother, who until now had always made a gay and funny story out of her wedding. An old snapshot came to Barbara's mind. Her parents had posed in front of the chapel in the army camp, which they had always described as being in the middle of nowhere. Their father, then Corporal MacLane, looked young, and his ears loomed large beneath his raw GI haircut—he had not yet begun to lose his hair. And their mother—how often the girls had poked fun at that snapshot. Her suit, which barely covered her knees, had the padded shoulders that were fashionable at that time, and her hair, brushed high in a pompadour in front, hung in fluff to her shoulders. Just like somebody in an old movie on TV, her daughters had often said. And those enormous shoulders, Mother, they had exclaimed whenever they saw the picture. You could have played football in the suit with all that padding.

Rosemary was not to be swayed. "Just because you couldn't have a wedding, Mother, is no reason why I should have one. I just want to get married in a suit without a lot of fuss and expense." She rose from the bed as if, as far as she was concerned, the matter was settled. "I'll go phone Aunt Josie and break the news, and then I simply have to study."

When Rosemary had gone into the kitchen to telephone, Barbara picked up the discarded wrapper from the seam tape and rolled it between her fingers. "What does Rosemary mean, an engagement ring is middle-class?"

"It's just one of those notions she has picked up at the University," said Mrs. MacLane. "Of course I wouldn't want her to go away to college and not get new ideas, but it is a little trying at times. She'll outgrow it. After all, my generation scoffed at a lot of things as being bourgeois."

Barbara did not like the suggestion that her sister was still young enough to outgrow an idea, as if it were a dress or a pair of shoes and she was a child. "Well, I just hope she hurries up and changes her mind about the kind of wedding she wants." Barbara wanted her sister to change her ideas, not outgrow them.

"I imagine she will," said Mrs. MacLane. "Rosemary really likes pretty clothes, even though she has taken to wearing drab colors since she has been going to the University. I only hope Gramma doesn't bring up her wedding veil."

"What wedding veil?" Barbara had never heard of such an heirloom in the family. "You mean she has a real wedding veil?"

"Oh, my, yes," answered Mr. MacLane. "Her own. A long one that calls for an elaborate wedding. I wasn't able to wear it for my wedding and Aunt Josie never married, so it has been packed away for over fifty years. I do hope Gramma has forgotten about it. You know how her memory is lately. Sometimes it's clear, and other times it's a little vague."

The veil, Barbara was certain, would be lace, yellow with age, and in her imagination it resembled an old lace curtain she and Rosemary had used for a veil when they were little girls playing bride. Barbara, who had pictured her sister floating down the aisle in a cloud of tulle, conceded that an old lace veil might be better than no veil at all, simply because it might persuade Rosemary to give up the idea of being married in a suit. Barbara fervently hoped that this was one of those days when her grandmother's memory would be clear. "You don't suppose she's going to be so practical, she'll want to get married in the city hall, do you?" asked Barbara, wishing Rosemary had assured her she would have a part in the wedding. "She might think it would save the gasoline it would take to drive to the church or something."

"She'd better not," said Mrs. MacLane. "Her father would put both feet down on any daughter of his who wanted to get married in the city hall."

Rosemary returned to the room. "Well, wouldn't you know," she announced. "Aunt Josie is all in a dither, and she and Gramma are going to rush right over. I tried to tell her I had to study sometime today, but you know Aunt Josie. She just doesn't listen."

"That means lunch." Mrs. MacLane folded the coat and laid it aside. "You go study until they get here, and I'll have your father drive you back to school as soon as lunch is over."

"If I can escape Aunt Josie," said Rosemary.

"Now, Rosemary, you mustn't mind your Aunt Josie. I know she's difficult, but she loves you," said Mrs. MacLane.

"I know," said Rosemary with a sigh. "Sometimes I feel she loves me to pieces."

"And you will find," added Mrs. MacLane dryly, "that being loved bears certain obligations whether you like it or not." Then she left to investigate her kitchen cupboards to see what she could produce for lunch on such short notice.

"Maybe I can do a little work before Aunt Josie and Gramma get here. I'm doing a paper on 'Plato: Teacher and Theorist,'" said Rosemary, picking up her books. "Millions of footnotes, when all I want to do is think about Greg."

It was not long before Aunt Josie's little car was heard turning into the driveway, and through the window Barbara saw Aunt Josie climb out and hurry around to the other side to assist Gramma out of the car before she could get out by herself. The whole family worried for fear Gramma might fall and break her hip someday. She *would* wear those high heels, much too high for an old lady. Someone had once told her she had a trim ankle, and Gramma still had her pride.

Aunt Josie, thin and nervous as a windshield wiper, was both fashionable and efficient. Today Barbara noticed, as she opened the front door, that Aunt Josie was wearing a pair of chopsticks, poked crisscross through her chignon. Aunt Josie, who was the buyer for the corset department in the largest store in the county, always tried to be a little bit different.

"Hello, Barbara dear," greeted Aunt Josie, and kissed her niece. "How nice to see you." Then her eye, accurate as a tape measure, appraised Barbara's appearance, and she gave her a little pat. "You must come to the store sometime. We have a nice little garment that would do wonders for you." Fortunately Aunt Josie did not expect an immediate answer. "Where's Rosemary?" she asked.

"Studying," answered Barbara, struggling to control her mingled feeling of amusement and irritation. A nice little garment! Well, she *had* eaten a lot of snick-erdoodles lately. Maybe they were beginning to show, but she did not intend to wear what her aunt called a "a nice little garment."

"Rosemary, darling!" cried Aunt Josie when Rose-mary came in, and she flew across the room to em-brace her niece. "I am so happy for you. A June bride! I just can't believe it. It seems only yesterday that you were sitting in your high chair spitting out strained carrots as fast as I could spoon them into your mouth."

Barbara observed that Rosemary was not particu-larly pleased at this picture of herself as an infant. About to become a married woman, she wanted to think of her childhood as something far away and half-forgotten.

"And how you used to love to have me bring empty boxes from the store for you to play with!" Aunt Josie went on.

Rosemary smiled gamely at the thought of herself playing happily among discarded corset boxes.

"Now tell us all about your young man," said Gramma, settling herself in a chair.

Buster strolled into the living room and sat down, twitching his elegant tail with displeasure. Buster did not care for visitors. They disturbed his rest. Barbara scooped up the cat and held him in her lap, where he regally consented to being petted. It was embarrass-ing to have a cat that so obviously disliked guests.

"And all about your wedding plans," added Aunt Josie. "I'm dying to hear about your wedding plans. An afternoon wedding is nicest. About a hundred guests, with a reception afterward at the Women's Club. And something different in the way of music. A little Bach perhaps while the guests are arriving and no Mendelssohn or Lohengrin for the marches. I am so tired of weddings that begin with dum *dum* de dum. It's no wonder so many brides drag their feet on the way to the altar. I do like a happy bride, one who looks as if she's glad to see the groom. And Betty—" here Aunt Josie turned to her sister —"I do hope you won't look like the cat that swallowed the canary. So often the mother of the bride does, while the mother of the groom struggles to hold back the tears." Aunt Josie was in good form.

"Now, Josie," said Gramma, "don't plan Rosemary's wedding for her."

"I'm not planning her wedding," protested Aunt Josie. "I was just making a few simple suggestions."

"I'm sure Rosemary hasn't had time to make up her mind about a lot of things," Mrs. MacLane said soothingly. "She's very busy with her studies, you know."

"Well, she'll soon be through with all that," said Gramma.

"No, Gramma," said Rosemary. "I'm going to finish college. Greg wants me to."

"We'll see." Gramma's mischievous smile implied that Rosemary would soon get over this ridiculous idea.

Rosemary became dignified. "Greg says I will be better equipped to be a wife and mother if I finish college."

"And I think he's right." Mrs. MacLane spoke quickly to head off any argument on the subject. "A girl who finishes college does make a better wife and mother. And I wouldn't want Rosemary ever to look back and regret missing it."

"And what does your young man do for a living?" asked Gramma.

"He's going to school, too," said Rosemary, "and he works in the Rad Lab part time—"

"What on earth is the Rad Lab?" interrupted Gramma.

"The Radiation Laboratory. That's where they smash the atoms," explained Rosemary. "Greg files things and goes to the library for the physicists. Things like that."

Both Aunt Josie and Gramma looked so disapproving that Rosemary quickly explained. "I don't mean he's going to make a career of filing things. He's working for his general secondary credential, and when he gets it he's going to teach History and English until we can save up enough money for him to go back to school and get his Master's degree and his Ph.D. His job doesn't pay an awful lot, but we can manage until he finishes school."

Neither Aunt Josie nor Gramma looked convinced. "It sounds like an ambitious program," said Aunt Josie skeptically.

"In my day," said Gramma, "young people didn't marry until they were ready to settle down."

"We will be settled down," said Rosemary earnestly. "We'll be settled down studying."

"We'll see about that," said Gramma roguishly.

Barbara tried desperately to think of some way to steer the conversation back to the wedding, but nothing came to mind.

Rosemary was still eager to defend Greg. "We will be studying," she insisted. "Greg wants me to make good grades." With anyone but Gramma she might have become angry, but now that Gramma was almost eighty, she was very sensitive about having her feelings hurt. The whole family had learned to tiptoe around Gramma's feelings.

"He must be a very strange young man," said Gramma. "When I was your age young men were interested in whether or not their wives were good cooks and housekeepers."

"He isn't strange at all." Rosemary was trying to be patient. "He's wonderful, and he says anyone who can read a cookbook can cook."

Gramma found this very funny. Even Mrs. MacLane smiled.

"Well, what is there to cooking but following directions?" demanded Rosemary, whose cheeks were beginning to turn pink. "Anybody can learn to cook with a little practice."

"It took me quite a while," said Gramma. "How I hated struggling with that old wood stove. It smoked every single morning, and every morning I wished we could move to the city, where we could have a gas stove. And I never could be sure of the temperature of the oven. 'Bake in a hot oven,' the recipes would say, but I was never sure how hot a hot oven was supposed to feel to my hand. The lopsided cakes your grandfather ate! Don't tell me anybody who can read can cook. I know better."

There was a moment of embarrassment until Mrs. MacLane said gently, "Now, Mother, things were different when you were a bride. Rosemary won't be learning to cook on a wood stove, and these days ovens have thermostats."

"And in a pinch they can always eat frozen foods," said Barbara helpfully. She did not want Gramma to think Rosemary and Greg need go hungry, just because Rosemary was not a very good cook.

Gramma sank, almost crumpled, back in her chair. She suddenly looked tired, as if she was feeling as old as she really was. "Yes, of course, things have changed since I was a bride. I keep forgetting. It really doesn't seem so long ago that I was struggling with that wood stove."

Barbara, who felt as if she would never be any older than she was at sixteen, was sorry for her old grandmother. Still, she had to hand it to her. Gramma was a game old lady in her high heels.

"Don't worry, Gramma," said Rosemary, also sensing her grandmother's feelings of age. "I won't let Greg starve."

"I'm sure you won't, my dear," said Gramma.

"And I really can cook a few things." Rosemary smiled at her grandmother. "Hamburgers and meat loaf and baked potatoes."

"Your grandfather always liked a bowl of oatmeal for breakfast," reminisced Gramma. "He said it stuck to his ribs."

Rosemary looked doubtful. "I don't know whether Greg likes oatmeal or not, but I'm sure I could learn to cook it."

Barbara admired her sister for tactfully not telling her grandmother she herself detested oatmeal. Or maybe it wasn't tact at all. Maybe it was love. Maybe Rosemary really would learn to cook oatmeal if Greg wanted it. Rosemary, cooking oatmeal of all things, and early in the morning, too. Rosemary, who always had such a hard time waking up. Barbara smiled to herself. She wondered if Rosemary would learn to eat oatmeal to keep Greg company. That would be the test of love, Rosemary eating oatmeal.

"Speaking of eating," said Aunt Josie, "have you had time to choose your silver pattern yet? You must be sure to register it at one of the local jewelers, so your friends will know what pieces to give you for wedding presents."

"Oh, we aren't going to have silver," said Rosemary.

"No silver!" Aunt Josie looked most disapproving. "What on earth are you going to eat with? Your fingers?"

"Stainless steel," answered Rosemary. "Greg and I feel that there are many handsome patterns in stainless steel and more important things to do in life than polish silver."

This produced complete silence from the older women, Barbara understood. She did not like to polish silver either. On the other hand, there were such pretty silverware patterns in all the women's magazines. It seemed a shame. . . . It would be such fun to open packages from the jewelry store. Oh well, Rosemary probably classed silverware as *things*, and as long as she could be persuaded to have a real wedding, Barbara was willing to concede her stainless steel instead of silver.

Rosemary was oblivious to the disapproving quality of the silence. "And Greg knows the most wonderful couple who make pottery on their own potter's wheel. They fire it and everything. We're going to commission them to make us a set of dishes. Greg says that in our own small way we will be patrons of the arts."

The older women were not just silent. They were speechless. Don't let them laugh, thought Barbara suddenly, please don't let them laugh. Rosemary is so serious.

"We thought we could have something in warm earth tones," Rosemary continued, unaware of the astonished silence she had created. "And I can make place mats out of burlap. Greg says burlap has a very handsome texture. And it's inexpensive." This was the new, practical Rosemary speaking.

She's overdoing it all the way, thought Barbara. No pretty dishes, no pastel linens, that practical suit. The whole thing, from Barbara's point of view, was beginning to sound just plain dreary. If this went on, she and Greg would probably spend their honeymoon picketing something.

It was Gramma who spoke first. "What nonsense!" she snapped, sitting up straight, no longer appearing crumbled in her chair. Gramma in her old age was often less tender of other people's feelings than they were of hers. "No matter how you look at it, burlap is still gunnysack material."

"Surely, Rosemary, you want some pretty things," said Aunt Josie. "Of course you do. Every bride does."

Barbara now foresaw another hazard to a pretty wedding. Aunt Josie could make Rosemary stubborn. She often had that effect on her relatives. There was no telling what the wedding would be like if that happened. Rosemary would probably get so practical, she wouldn't even want a new suit. She would probably wear that blue one she had bought for Easter two years ago.

"Earth tones, indeed!" sputtered Gramma. "Dirt-colored is more like it. If you think I'm going to waste my money giving you any clunky old pottery that scratches the table, you are mistaken."

"Now, Mother," said Mrs. MacLane, "Rosemary really hasn't had time to think over what she really wants. There is plenty of time for her to decide before the wedding."

Now Rosemary was injured. "Mother, I'm not a child. Greg and I know what we want."

"Of course she'll change her mind," said Aunt Josie briskly.

Inevitably Rosemary began to look stubborn. It was her wedding, and she was not going to have her relatives tell her what to do with it. She had stood her ground against Greg's mother; she could stand her ground against her Aunt Josie.

"Of course she will change her mind," said Gramma, "and she will choose a pretty china pattern, too."

"Now, Mother. It is her wedding, you know," said Mrs. MacLane gently. "Each generation has to be a little bit different. Otherwise the world would come to a standstill."

And there was Gramma looking crumpled and piti-
ful again. "Of course it is her wedding," she said with
a sigh. "But I don't know what gets into girls these
days. They seem to be afraid of pretty things. Well, I
guess the world is changing. Young men didn't smash
atoms in my day either."

Barbara considered her grandmother thoughtfully.
If she was upset now, wait until she heard what came
next. The suit.

"Now, Mother, don't you worry," said Aunt Josie.
"We'll give Rosemary a lovely wedding, and she will
be the prettiest bride you ever saw."

I hope she will, thought Barbara fervently, that suit
looming before her. I hope we have a pretty bride
with at least one pretty attendant. That was all she
asked.

"The box!" said Gramma, suddenly sitting up on the
edge of the chair. "I completely forgot about the box.
I got it out of the closet and put it out where I would
be sure to remember it, and than I came away without it. I declare, my memory is getting worse every
day." She sank back, worried and disappointed.

"I brought it," said efficient Aunt Josie. "It's out in
the back of the car."

"Run and get it," ordered Gramma, for the moment
forgetting that her daughter was a grown woman and
not a child.

"What box?" asked Rosemary, when Aunt Josie had
gone out to the car.

"You'll see," said Gramma with a smile.

Barbara, who was sure she knew what was in the box,
glanced at her mother and saw that she looked tired
and resigned.

In a moment Aunt Josie returned with a large suit
box, which she laid on her mother's lap. The family
waited while Gramma's gnarled and trembling fingers
picked at the knots in the string. Finally she was able

to lift the lid and lay it on the floor, and her old hands folded back the tissue paper, brittle with age, and revealed the folds of a wedding veil.

"Why, Grammal" gasped Rosemary.

"Oh." Barbara had never seen such lace. It was gossamer, scattered with flowers and bordered with the most delicate scallops. And she had pictured it looking something like an old lace curtain.

"I've saved it over fifty years. . . ." Gramma fumbled for her handkerchief.

Barbara was beginning to see what her mother meant by a wedding's being an occasion for sentiment. Something old, something new, something borrowed, something blue. . . . If Rosemary disapproved of sentiment, how would she react to this?

Gramma wiped the corner of her eye. One of her daughters had not married at all, the other had had a wartime wedding in an army camp, while Gramma's veil had lain in its tissue paper for over half a century.

Barbara suddenly felt a little sad herself. Poor old Gramma with her memories. It was so sad to see her sitting there with her wedding veil on her lap, not knowing that modern, unsentimental Rosemary was going to disappoint her. Barbara glanced at her mother. The anxious crease between her brows showed the distress in her mind. She did not want to see her mother, who was almost eighty, disappointed, but neither did she want a wedding in keeping with the veil.

"Father gave me a beautiful wedding, even though I was marrying a poor boy," said Gramma, as her shaky hands lifted the veil, creamy with age, from the box. "Of course that was before he lost his money on mining and streetcar stocks. I had six bridesmaids and two flower girls." She unfolded the veil, let it fall to the floor, and sat looking at it, her face soft with memory.

I can't bear it, thought Barbara, unable to look at her sister. It was all so sad and sentimental. She blinked back her tears. Poor old Gramma.

She wanted to reassure her grandmother by saying, I'll wear it, Gramma. I'll wear it when my turn comes. As she watched her mother and Aunt Josie help to spread the veil, her thoughts flew to Bill Cunningham, whom she had not had a chance to mention to Rosemary. If in a month or two they began to go steady and went steady for a year and then got engaged and were engaged for a year, by that time she would be as old as Rosemary was now. . . . Buster jumped down from her lap and stalked across the room to investigate this strange new thing.

"Barbara, put that cat out." Mrs. MacLane spoke so crisply that the contrast between her words and the atmosphere of the room was a relief to Barbara, who willingly opened the door and shoved Buster out.

"It is real princess lace," said Aunt Josie. "You just don't see lace like that anymore."

Rosemary bent over to examine the veil, holding her hands, with her fingers spread, beneath it, so they appeared to be seen through a creamy mist.

Tell Gramma about the suit, Barbara mentally pleaded with her sister. Tell her and get it over. Don't let her get her hopes up.

"It's beautiful," said Rosemary softly. "Just beautiful." Rosemary smiled at her grandmother. "Thank you, Gramma. Thank you for saving it for me."

Barbara, standing beside her sister, threw her arms around Rosemary and hugged her. She hugged her for her kindness to Gramma, she hugged her for being sentimental, she hugged her because she was so happy. No bride could wear a veil like Gramma's with a suit. And no bride in such a veil could walk down the aisle unattended.

Chapter Seven

Barbara and Bill were sitting on the front steps of the MacLane house with a plate of butterscotch refrigerator cookies between them. This time Barbara had hidden the cooky canister in her closet, so Gordy could not find it and eat up all the cookies before Bill brought her home from school on his Vespa. Barbara had been telling Bill about Rosemary and Greg and how they planned to continue school after they were married.

"Good cookies," said Bill, reaching for another.

"Thank you," answered Barbara. How nice he looked with his shirt open at the throat—tanned, healthy, confident.

"You're a good cook," said Bill.

Barbara smiled modestly. The cookies had been bought already mixed and chilled at the supermarket. All she had to do was peel off the plastic wrapper, slice them, and bake them. She was taking chemistry, and there was, after all, a limit to the number of cookies she had time to bake, even for Bill Cunningham.

"I think you should kiss me," said Bill suddenly.

With effort Barbara managed to hide her startled feelings. Was he joking? Or did Bill really want to kiss her? "What for?" Barbara appeared calm, a little detached, as if kissing Bill was an impersonal matter she could consider and either accept or reject on its merits. Actually she was thinking, Kiss Bill? Here? On the front steps in front of the whole neighborhood?

"It's our anniversary," said Bill, as if he was reminding her.

"How stupid of me to have forgotten," said Barbara, stalling for time to find out if Bill was only joking. "Which anniversary do you mean?".

"Don't tell me you have forgotten so soon." Bill shook his head. "It was just two weeks ago today that the sound truck played our song."

"Of course. *Chattanooga Choochoo*," cried Barbara, flattered that he had remembered the exact day. "Our second anniversary! How could I have forgotten?" She glanced hastily up and down the street, and when she saw no one, she closed her eyes, tilted back her head, and leaned across the cooky plate toward Bill. His lips barely brushed hers, and when she opened her eyes he was grinning at her. To her annoyance, she felt color rising to her cheeks. It was embarrassing to be betrayed by her blushes when she had meant to carry off the whole incident with careless gaiety. "Have another cooky," she said with calculated nonchalance.

"Thanks, I believe I will."

From inside the house came the sound of the television set, and Barbara wondered uneasily if Gordy had been looking out the front window a moment ago. Well, what if he had? It had been an innocent kiss, scarcely a kiss at all. Still, the knowledge that Gordy might have been watching took some of the pleasure out of the moment. For once she hoped he had been in the kitchen eating beans out of a tin can.

When Bill had eaten the last cooky and had ridden off down the hill on his motor scooter, Barbara took the mail out of the mailbox, noticed with interest that there was a letter on good-quality paper for her mother from Greg's mother, and stepped into the living room. Gordy was not there. Only Buster sat in front of the television set, his crossed eyes staring fascinated at a cartoon program. "Gordy!" she called out. "Are you planning to watch this program?"

"No," Gordy called back from his room. "I turned it on for Buster."

Barbara snapped off the set, and Buster fixed her with his evil eyes. "Oh, you," she said crossly. She held the envelope from Greg's mother up to the light, but she could not read a word. She tossed it onto a table beside an envelope covered with figures in her mother's writing, which she picked up and examined curiously. It was a rough list of wedding expenses. The total shocked Barbara. She had no idea a wedding cost *this* much. The wedding dress, flowers . . . all the items that had never occurred to her . . . the organist's fee, postage for wedding invitations. Beside the list of wedding expenses was another column of figures. Life insurance, car insurance, health insurance, car payments. The total of this column also shocked Barbara. No wonder her mother had hoped Gramma would forget about her wedding veil.

Gordy appeared in the door of his room, his guitar in hand. "What did you go and turn that TV off for?" he demanded.

"Wasting TV on a *cat*." Barbara was scornful.

"Buster likes cartoons," said Gordy. "Cats get bored the same as people."

"Then he should be out catching mice or getting in cat fights or something," said Barbara. "He should do cat things, not people things."

Gordy struck a jangling chord on his guitar. "I saw you smooching out in front with the Cunning Ham."

So Gordy had been watching. The thing to do was put him on the defensive as quickly as possible. "'Smooch.' What a quaint old-fashioned word," she said, displaying an amusement that she did not feel.

"It was quaint old-fashioned smooching." Gordy was not going to accept the defensive.

"Bill Cunningham and I were not smooching." Barbara enunciated each syllable clearly and distinctly. "And why don't you mind your own business?"

"Ha," said Gordy darkly. He disappeared into his room, where he began to sing, "Love, oh, love, oh, careless love."

That Gordy. Of all the millions and billions of thirteen-year-old boys in the world, why did she have to draw Gordy for a brother? And having drawn him, why did he have to be looking out the window at that particular instant? She wondered if he was going to tell her father and what she should say if he did. It would be difficult to explain that Bill's lips had barely brushed hers in what could scarcely be called a kiss. And if she tried to explain, her father was almost certain to say, "Define your terms. What is a kiss?" And then she would have to say, "When somebody touches somebody with his lips." And he would say, "It sounds to me as if you were kissing Bill Cunningham out on the front steps."

At this point the telephone rang, and Barbara went into the kitchen to answer it. Rosemary was calling. "Is Mother there?" She sounded as if she was in a hurry.

"Not yet," said Barbara. "She should be here any minute."

"Look," said Rosemary hurriedly. "Tell Mother to call me the minute she comes in. I've got a lot to say, and it's too hard to collect enough change to make a long call from a pay phone."

"What happened?" Barbara was all eagerness for the latest development in Rosemary's life, and regretted that Rosemary never had enough change for a long telephone call.

"Greg's mother came over and took us to lunch." Rosemary sounded breathless, as she always did when she telephoned from school.

"What did she say?" Barbara asked eagerly.

"She was terribly nice and was so happy we had decided to have a real wedding, and she was positively thrilled about Gramma's veil. She said I really should choose silver and china patterns, because so many of their friends who lived in the East would want to know, and they could hardly send handmade pottery. We'd much rather have checks, so we could buy books and records, but you can't tell people that, so maybe she's right."

"Maybe," agreed Barbara, worrying about her mother's list of expenses. "Does she still expect us to send out two hundred invitations?"

"No. She said she was writing Mother that she was revising her list and cutting it to the bone," continued Rosemary. "And she said we really must start planning the wedding. She says a wedding must be organized, or everybody goes to pieces at the last minute and nobody enjoys it. So I think I'd better talk to Mother about wedding plans. And she—oops! My time is up. Good-by." Rosemary hung up with a clatter.

"Good-by," said Barbara to the dead telephone. At least Rosemary had agreed that they should start planning. Now, after she and her mother had been trying to get her to settle down and plan the wedding ever since Rosemary had announced that she was going to get married in June. She glanced at the cooky canister that she had forgotten to hide again before she had taken the plate of cookies out to Bill. It was empty. Even Gordy could not have eaten that many cookies at once, so he must be stockpiling them in his room for the future. She was trying to decide whether she should accost Gordy and demand her cookies back or avoid a battle and bake another batch, when her mother came through the back door with her usual armload of groceries.

"The pounds of food it takes to keep this family going!" Mrs. MacLane was glad to relieve her arms of the weight of the groceries.

"Mother, there's a letter for you from Greg's mother. Rosemary has had lunch with her, and now she says we have to start planning the wedding right away. She asked me to tell you to phone her the instant you came in." Barbara started to unpack one of the bags.

"Oh, she does, does she?" asked Mrs. MacLane dryly. "It's nice to know that her future mother-in-law has such an influence over her."

Barbara went into the living room for Mrs. Aldredge's letter, which she handed her mother. Mrs. MacLane laid a box of macaroni on the counter, opened the letter, and read it while Barbara watched. When she had finished the letter, Mrs. MacLane glanced at the typewritten list of names and addresses that was enclosed. "Well . . ." was all she said.

"Well what?" asked Barbara.

"Well, at least she has cut her list in half. That's a help, but there are still our friends to invite, too." Mrs. MacLane looked worried. "I talked to your Aunt Josie this morning, and she says that even if we get the wedding dress through her store, using her discount, a dress that will go with Gramma's veil would cost over a hundred dollars. And I suppose now we'll have to have a caterer. . . . I do want Rosemary to have a nice wedding, but I honestly don't see where that much money is coming from."

"I'll put the groceries away," offered Barbara. "You phone Rosemary. I got the impression she was going to hover over the phone until you called, because she's in such a hurry to get on with the wedding plans."

Mrs. MacLane took a pad of paper and a pencil

from the drawer by the telephone before she put through the call to Rosemary. Barbara moved quietly about the kitchen, so she would not miss a word.

"Hello, Rosemary? . . . Yes. Yes, I received the letter and the list. . . . Yes, I know, dear. I know you have finals coming up, but if you stop to think, so does everyone in the family, and your father is responsible for the printing of the yearbook. You know what a chore that is at this time of year." Mrs. MacLane doodled a wedding cake on the pad of paper while Rosemary talked. "Yes, dear, I realize you have to write a paper on Plato, but after all, it is your wedding, and you are the only one who can make some of these decisions."

Decisions like who is to be the maid of honor, thought Barbara, carefully folding a paper bag that was the right size for carrying a lunch.

"All right," said Mrs. MacLane. "You are going to wear Gramma's wedding veil. That much we have settled. . . . I know you'd rather wear a short dress, dear, but you can't wear a short dress with a long veil. It wouldn't look right. Now how many attendants do you want?"

Barbara held her breath.

"Yes, dear. Barbara for your maid of honor." Mrs. MacLane jotted a note on the pad of paper while Barbara felt light-headed with relief. "And now who else? . . . Yes, Millie and Greg's sister Anne. And what about your cousin Elinor? You know Uncle Charlie will be hurt if you don't include her."

Even Barbara could hear Rosemary's wail over the telephone.

"Now, Rosemary," said Mrs. MacLane, "I know she's only twelve, but she can be a junior bridesmaid."

Oh, dear, thought Barbara. Elinor was at the chunky stage, where she appeared to have no waistline. She was painfully self-conscious, and she giggled. Oh, how she giggled, especially when boys were mentioned. Barbara could picture her walking down the aisle, her lips compressed in an effort to hold back the giggles, her bouquet quivering. Barbara could understand Rosemary's wail of protest, so loud even she could hear it. A junior bridesmaid who went off into a gale of uncontrollable giggles during the ceremony would certainly spoil the wedding. And then Barbara, avid reader of wedding news, had an inspiration. "Mother," she whispered urgently.

"Just a minute, Rosemary." Mrs. MacLane held the phone against her shoulder. "What is it, Barbara?"

"Elinor could circulate the guest book at the reception. Lots of wedding stories in the paper mention a girl who circulates the guest book. That would give her something to do."

Mrs. MacLane relayed this suggestion to the bride, who thought this a perfect solution. Circulating the guest book would make Elinor feel part of the wedding party, and she would be less prone to giggles if she did not feel that everyone was looking at her.

"And what about the reception?" inquired Mrs. MacLane, now that cousin Elinor was disposed of.

The buzz of Rosemary's voice through the telephone receiver was rapid. Apparently she knew what she wanted in the way of a wedding reception. Barbara strained to catch even one word.

"I think that's a very wise decision," said Mrs. MacLane. "Punch and cake at the church will be easy for everyone. And if the weather is pleasant, as it probably will be, we can have it outdoors. The Sunday-school room is a little dark, although I'm sure flowers would help it."

There went a catered reception, thought Barbara, glad this strain on the family budget was eliminated. An outdoor reception in the garden of the church would be much prettier—flowers and pink punch and light dresses against the background of old redwood trees, the afternoon sun filtering through the branches, a bird singing—no, skip the bird. The picture was getting too sentimental.

"As near as I can make out," said Mrs. MacLane, when her conversation was finished, "what Rosemary wants is a do-it-yourself wedding. She doesn't want a caterer or a florist to decorate the church. She wants us to gather flowers for the church ourselves, although just where we are to gather them she doesn't make clear. She says the things we do ourselves are the most beautiful. Except for the cake. It seems that all her life she has looked at wedding cakes in the window of Larson's Bakery and dreamed of seeing her own there someday."

"Oh," said Barbara, interested that her sister was revealing sentimental feelings, "does she want a do-it-yourself wedding dress, too?"

"If she does, she will have to be talked out of it," said Mrs. MacLane. "She isn't the only one in the family who has finals. Come on, let's get out the wedding veil again and see what kind of dress might go with it that we can afford."

Barbara was only too happy to agree. Naturally they would want to see what the veil looked like on a bride, and naturally she would be the one to try it on. As they walked down the hall past Gordy's room, Gordy burst into song. "Love, oh love, oh careless love." Barbara glared.

"That's a pretty song," said Mrs. MacLane, pausing at Gordy's door. "I like it much better than that gloomy one you've been singing about twenty-nine links of chain around your leg. Why don't you sing it more often?"

'O.K., Mom, I will." Gordy grinned at Barbara, who

wanted to hit him over the head with his guitar. "Sorrow, sorrow, to my heart," he sang with gusto. "Sorrow, sorrow, to my heart."

Once again Barbara wondered why, of all the thirteen-year-old boys in the world, she had to have this particular one for a brother. And even though he stopped singing, the words of his song continued to ring through her head.

In the bedroom Barbara and her mother took down the suit box from the closet shelf, set it on her bed, and removed the lid. Gently they lifted out the veil and spread it out on Rosemary's bed, which was not cluttered with stuffed animals.

"It is lovely," admitted Mrs. MacLane. "I don't blame Rosemary for wanting to wear it."

"It's awfully long." Barbara was waiting for her mother to ask her to try it on, the veil she would wear for her own wedding someday.

"There is no possible way that it could be worn with a short dress. It needs a dress with a train. And Rosemary simply can't wear a long satin dress in June in California. It would be much too warm."

"Isn't a dress with a train awfully expensive?" asked Barbara doubtfully.

"I'm afraid so." Mrs. MacLane's brow wrinkled throughfully as she looked at the veil and considered its possibilities. "*Peau de soie* might be nice, but a dress with a train of any really nice fabric is going to cost more than we can afford."

"And that will mean long bridesmaid dresses, too," Barbara was saying, when suddenly Buster ran into the room and, in one flying leap, landed in the middle of the fragile veil. His claws clutched the gossamer threads, and he rolled over on his back, ready to play the change the sheet game that Barbara played with him once a week.

Mrs. MacLane gasped. Barbara screamed and grabbed at the cat. Buster rolled over in the lace.

"Stop him!" cried Mrs. MacLane. "He's ruining it!"

Gordy stopped singing in the middle of a phrase and came to see what the commotion was all about. He stood staring, unable to say anything. Buster laid back his ears and with his strong hind legs kicked at Barbara through the lace. The old veil shredded.

"Do something," beseeched Barbara, struggling to hold Buster motionless within the lace. The claws of his hind feet scratched her hands.

"The beautiful old lace. . . ." Mrs. MacLane was in despair.

Gordy approached Buster cautiously. "Nice kitty," he said, petting his cat through the lace. Buster hesitated, stared at Gordy an instant, dismissed him, and went on kicking with his hind legs.

"Nice kitty!" Barbara was bitter as she handed the whole lacy, kicking bundle to her brother. How anyone could call this demon, this fur-covered fiend, nice. . . .

Gordy ignored his sister as he continued to pet Buster. "Relax, boy," he said soothingly.

"What will we tell Gramma?" Mrs. MacLane wondered aloud. "She'll be heartbroken, simply heartbroken."

Gordy stroked Buster through the lace. Now he had his cat's attention, because the animal stopped kicking, with his ears laid back and his tail lashing, he looked watchfully at Gordy. "Nice kitty," crooned Gordy. "Nice old boy." Gently he began to unhook the cruel claws from the threads.

"Maybe if I opened the refrigerator door he'd want to run into the kitchen," suggested Barbara.

"Oh no, that would be worse," said Mrs. MacLane. "He'd jump down and tear the lace even more."

"Nice kitty." Gordy ignored his mother and sister.
"Nice puss." Buster's hind feet were disentangled from
the lace. Carefully Gordy unhooked it from a front
paw. Buster was not entirely convinced he wanted
this delightful game to end. He laid back his ears and
extended the claws of his front paws in ten cruel arcs.

Barbara moaned. Her sister's wedding, to say nothing of her own, ruined by an evil cat. And she had not
even had a chance to try on the veil.

"Come on, Buster," coaxed Gordy. Buster slowly
sheathed his claws, but kept a wary eye on Gordy.
"How would you like some cat tuna, huh, Buster?"
Through the lace he rubbed Buster's nose, and Buster
became less wary. He enjoyed having his black-satin
nose rubbed. He raised his head as if to say, Do it
some more. Gordy unhooked the last claw and carefully lifted the cat free of the veil.

"You get that horrible cat out of here," stormed Barbara. "Why Mother and Dad let you keep that awful
beast is beyond me. He claws everything to shreds.
My stuffed animals, the furniture, everything. Someday he'll claw the whole house down over our heads
in splinters, and then I hope you will be satisfied!"

"Relax, Barbed Wire," drawled Gordy. "Who let him
play with the sheets in the first place?" And with
Buster draped over his arm Gordy left the room.

Barbara felt suddenly deflated. Gordy was right.
She had let Buster play on the bed when she was
changing the cheets. She had even encouraged him.
Naturally he had thought the wedding veil was some
new kind of sheet and that she would be willing to
play with him. It was all her own fault.

"What's done is done," said Mrs. MacLane sadly.
"Let's see how much damage there is. Perhaps it can
be mended."

Carefully Barbara helped her mother spread the
veil on the bed once more, and together they stood

looking at the damage. In the center of the veil were three jagged holes, two large and one small, and these were surrounded by little breaks and tears. They both could see that it was hopeless. The veil could never be mended.

"It's ruined," was Barbara's blunt pronouncement. She added bitterly, "And now that she doesn't have a veil to wear I suppose Rosemary will go back to her original idea of a practical wedding in a Harris-tweed suit."

Mrs. MacLane managed a rueful little laugh. "She didn't say she planned to be married in a tweed suit, Barbara. That is an exaggeration."

"And what about my wedding?" demanded Barbara. "That old tomcat has spoiled my wedding, too."

"We'll worry about your wedding when we come to it." Mrs. MacLane fingered the wedge of the veil. "It's a long way off."

"I'm only two years younger than Rosemary," Barbara reminded her mother.

"Don't you start getting any ideas," said Mrs. MacLane mildly, her eyes on the veil.

Barbara did not say anything. How surprised her mother would be if she knew that only a little while ago Bill Cunningham had kissed her, sort of.

"You know," said Mrs. MacLane suddenly, "I do believe all our problems are solved!"

"By a tattered veil?" Barbara was skeptical.

"Yes," answered her mother. "The veil is only damaged in the center. This end could be made into a very lovely short veil, fingertip length, by cutting it here and gathering the cut edge onto a band or a spray of orange blossoms or something of the sort."

Barbara could visualize this. The lace was so fine and so light it would make a very beautiful short veil.

"And the other end," continued Mrs. MacLane, "and the part on either side of the holes could be made into a little jacket to wear over a simple wedding dress. See, the back and front could be cut here and the sleeves there, so that the scallops of the edge of the veil would make the edge of the jacket."

"Mother, that's a marvelous idea!" cried Barbara. "Lots of wedding dresses have little jackets. I read about them in the paper all the time. And that way Rosemary can wear a short dress and so can the rest of us!"

"And now that that is settled, let's put the veil away before anything else happens to it." Mrs. MacLane spoke briskly. "It's time to start dinner."

"What about Gramma?" asked Barbara, as they folded the tattered veil and returned it to the suit box. "What do you think she will say?"

"Your grandmother, even though she is old and her feelings are easily hurt, is a woman of character who has survived many disappointments in her lifetime," said Mrs. MacLane, "and although she will be upset when she hears what happened, I am sure she will be happy that enough of her veil was saved for Rosemary to wear."

Chapter Eight

After Buster's shredding of the wedding veil, hostility between brother and sister grew more intense. Barbara shoved Buster outside whenever she found the cat in the house. "You're just an old nuisance!" she would say, and slam the door. Then Gordy would begin to sing *Careless Love* in an irritating way that Barbara felt amounted to blackmail.

At the same time plans for the wedding went ahead, and because most of the planning was done by telephone, Barbara became quite openly an eavesdropper. Almost every evening Rosemary called with an order or a suggestion, and almost always the call ended abruptly when her twenty cents had run out. Then Mrs. MacLane would call her back so that the toll would go on the family's telephone bill. Aunt Josie came over several evenings to talk over the wedding. She was full of ideas. It was very smart this year for bridesmaids to carry garlands of ivy instead of flowers. And had Rosemary thought of having the wedding veil gathered onto a coronet?

And look like a ballerina about to dance *Swan Lake*, Barbara thought privately. As for carrying a garland of ivy—she only hoped the matter would not be brought up again. It was always best to let Aunt Josie babble on and to hope that most of her ideas would fade away. Next Aunt Josie suggested blue polished cotton with bouquets of hydrangeas. Barbara, who wanted to carry flowers, not shrubbery, did not mind at all when this suggestion was forgotten.

Then one morning before school, while Barbara was pressing the full skirt she was wearing, without bothering to take it off, her mother announced, "The Amys want to give Rosemary a shower, and we thought next Saturday would be a good time. Rosemary is coming home, anyway, and there won't be many Saturdays before the wedding."

Barbara, who had lifted the front of her skirt over the end of the ironing board and was trying to press it with the iron pointed toward herself, started to protest, Oh, Mother, not the Amys! but caught the words in time. Any shower was sure to be fun, and this was the moment to keep her opinion of the Amys as a group to herself. "Will I be invited?" she asked.

"Yes. You and Aunt Josie and Gramma, because you are family," said Mrs. MacLane. "Here, let me press the back of your skirt before you burn yourself."

The first party, and she would get to go, thought Barbara ecstatically, as she lifted the back of her skirt over the ironing board and her mother began to run the iron over it. Fun, excitement, presents—lots of presents, because there were at least twenty-five Amys—good things to eat, although half of the Amys would protest that really they shouldn't, they simply had to lose a few pounds. Barbara could hardly wait for Saturday to come. "Which Amy is giving the shower?" she asked, pulling her pressed skirt from the ironing board and feeling it warm against the back of her legs.

"Nancy Bodger," said Mrs. MacLane. "Dessert and coffee. And it's to be a miscellaneous shower. We thought you could make up some sort of excuse about wanting to see Tootie about some homework and ask Rosemary to walk over to the Bodgers' with you."

"Mother!" groaned Barbara. "Of all the awful ideas! I try to *avoid* Tootie."

"Well, I can't tell Nancy that," Mrs. MacLane pointed out. "And, anyway, Tootie probably won't even be home. I can't imagine a boy his age wanting to hang around the house when his mother's friends are there."

This was true. "But Rosemary will know something is up, because she knows how I feel about Tootie," Barbara reminded her mother.

"We'll just have to hope for the best," answered her mother. "I'll leave that part of it up to you. It is practically impossible to surprise a bride with a shower, so there's no point in worrying about it."

The plans for the shower rolled along during the week. All the Amys wanted to know what Rosemary might like for a shower gift, and the MacLanes' phone rang several times a day. It seemed to Barbara that her mother found unnecessary amusement in every conversation. "As near as I can figure out," she would say, "Rosemary likes anything that is modern, earth-colored, and clunky. You know, artsy-craftsy." Or she might say, "Pink bath towels! Don't you know pink is too old-fashioned for this generation. Pumpkin color is the thing. Or brown or olive green." Or, "Sometimes I think they don't want dishes at all. I think they plan to eat off phonograph records."

"Oh, Mother!" Barbara would then protest. "How silly can you get?" But when she answered the telephone herself and an Amy inquired of her what colors Rosemary was collecting for her kitchen and bathroom, she could only say lamely, "Well . . . she likes earth-colored dishes and pumpkin-colored towels."

"Earth-colored dishes!" the Amy invariably exclaimed.

"Yes," Barbara would say defensively, "she and

Greg know a potter over in Berkeley who is going to make them a set of plates."

"Oh . . ." was the Amy's usual answer. "Well . . . perhaps I should get her something for her kitchen."

Since Barbara was to be a guest at the shower she, too, was faced with the problem of a gift. She shopped after school one day, even though it meant missing a ride home on Bill's Vespa. As she wandered through the shops, everything seemed too flowery, too fragile, or too pastel for Rosemary's taste, but finally in a store specializing in imported furniture and gifts she found a pair of squat terra-cotta candlesticks from Mexico. They seemed to fill all the requirements, and were earth-colored, amusing, and just right for a bride and groom whom she could see dining by candlelight. Gradually the picture in her mind faded and re-emerged—Barbara and Bill were dining by candle-light. They were students at the University; they had an apartment near the campus. . . .

Early Saturday afternoon Rosemary arrived in her usual confusion of books and laundry, but this time there was a difference. Rosemary was wearing an en-gagement ring.

"Rosemary!" cried Barbara, seizing her sister's hand as soon as its sparkle caught her eye. "Where did you get that ring?"

Rosemary laughed. "From Greg, of course, silly. Who else would be giving me a ring?"

"But—" Barbara held her tongue. It would not do to remind her sister that a short time ago she had dis-missed an engagement ring as middle-class. Just be glad she changed her mind, Barbara told herself. "It's beautiful," she said. And it was. It was a large stone, full of fire and light, in a plain gold setting. She wished she could keep from wondering how Greg could afford such a ring.

"It was Greg's grandmother's." Rosemary might have read Barbara's thoughts. "His mother got it out of the safe-deposit box and brought it over to him. He gave it to me last night after the library closed. Isn't it beautiful?" She held out her hand and whirled around, as if her ring trailed light behind it like a Fourth-of-July sparkler.

Barbara could hold her tongue no longer. "I thought engagement rings were middle-class."

"Not if they are heirlooms," was Rosemary's airy explanation.

"Boy. Some hunk of ice," said Gordy, who had come into the room in time to overhear the conversation. "Doing anything special tonight, Rosie?"

Barbara shot him a look that said, You be quiet! Honestly, Gordy actually worked at being exasperating.

"Just studying. Greg is working tonight." Rosemary was so preoccupied with her own affairs that she missed this bit of family byplay.

She had a hem that needed repairing, poetry that had to be read for English, and work that must, simply must, be done on that paper on "Plato: Teacher and Theorist." She had to turn it in by next Wednesday. The professor was an old bear about late papers. She hoped someone had found time to address wedding invitations. *Please* no little figures on top of the cake. She and Greg had agreed on that. No cardboard wedding bells, either. Just a little nosegay of real flowers to match her wedding bouquet. That much she was sure of. And could Barbara be an angel and find time to type the first part of her paper on Plato? She had a few pages written. They were full of footnotes, which were a nuisance to type, but everybody knew professors adored footnotes, especially if there were a few in French or German. Unfortunately hers were all in English.

"You don't sound very thirsty for knowledge," Barbara observed.

"Of course I'm thirsty for knowledge," retorted Rosemary. "It's just that . . . well, you know. Plato, when I'm planning a wedding."

It's a good thing the footnotes are in English, thought Barbara, who would much prefer addressing wedding invitations or even doing her own homework to typing a paper on Plato. But type she did, rolling the platen of the typewriter up each time she typed a number to indicate a footnote at the bottom of the page, and then forgetting to leave space for the footnote at the bottom of the paper and having to do the page all over again. It was a tiresome chore, doubly tiresome because she was anticipating the shower. She was glad when evening came.

After dinner Rosemary put on an old housecoat and some woolly bedroom slippers she had left behind when she went away to college and settled down at her desk to attack Plato. She was working so hard, she did not notice that her mother changed her dress and left the house. As Barbara was changing her own dress, she said as casually as she could manage, "Come on, Rosemary, put on a dress and walk over to the Bodgers' house with me. I have to borrow a book from Tootie."

"Can't," answered Rosemary.

This was not encouraging. Barbara pushed the zipper on the back of her dress up as far as she could and then reached down over her shoulder and pulled it up the rest of the way, while she considered what to say next that would not spoil the surprise for Rosemary. "Please, Rosemary. I simply have to get the book, and you know how Dad is about my going out alone at night."

"Can't Mom drive you? I'll be up half the night as it is."

Barbara looked at her sister's head bent over the circle of light from the study lamp. There was no question about it. She was a problem bride. First she was determined to be practical about her wedding. Now she had to study. "Mom's gone out on an errand." As a last resort Barbara could come right out and tell her sister she had to go, because she was about to be the guest of honor at a shower, but only as a last resort. She tried again, and endeavored to keep the urgency out of her voice. "You've been grubbing on Plato all afternoon. You need some fresh air."

"Can't, I said."

Barbara was getting desperate. The minutes were slipping away, and she was committed to deliver Rosemary to the Bodgers' front door by eight o'clock. "If you're going to study late you'll want a snack. We could stop for a malt or something." Her voice was more pleading than she had intended.

Rosemary finally looked up from her desk. "Did you know," she asked, "that one peanut will provide enough energy for a student to study all evening?"

That was Rosemary. A scientific answer to everything now that she had gone away to college. "No, I didn't," said Barbara crossly. "And what is more, I don't believe it. I get hungry when I study."

"Psychic boredom," pronounced Rosemary. "You don't want to study, so you decide you are hungry. All you need is one peanut."

Barbara was so exasperated with her sister, she felt close to tears. "Oh, you and your psychology. Or, rather, your roommate's psychology. All I'm asking is that you come on one little errand with me." Then she added virtuously, "After all, I have been typing for you."

Rosemary looked quizzically at her sister. "How come you are borrowing a book from Tootie Bodger?" she wanted to know.

"I need it," answered Barbara. "You'll have to come with me."

"Out of thirty-five students in what class it is, and you have to borrow a book from Tootie?" Rosemary raised an eyebrow and smiled. "There's something funny going on around here."

"Well. . . ."

"And Mom has gone out?" persisted Rosemary.

"Yes."

Rosemary laughed and dropped her pencil on her desk. "I get it."

"Get what?" Barbara managed wide-eyed innocence.

Doubt flickered across Rosemary's face. "At least I think I do. Are the Amys meeting tonight?"

"What makes you think they are?" countered Barbara, longing to glance at her watch. It must be time to go by now, and she had not even succeeded in getting Rosemary dressed. In a minute she would have to come right out and tell her.

"Because Mrs. Bodger is a pillar of the Amys, and Mom always does her errands in the day time, and you would never borrow a book from Tootie of your own free will. If you did, you'd get it after school instead of insisting that I go out in the evening." Rosemary left her desk and walked toward the closet. "It all adds up. I am about to be surprised by the Amys with a shower. Am I right?"

Barbara, who was applying lipstick, was not able to answer.

"Don't worry," said Rosemary cheerfully, as she pulled off her housecoat. "I'll be surprised."

At least I didn't tell, thought Barbara, relieved to see Rosemary dressing.

"Are we late?" asked Rosemary, as she combed and fluffed her hair.

"Not if we hurry," said Barbara, giving up pretense.

"Now remember," she said, when the two girls had left the house and had started the short walk to the Bodgers', "I'm supposed to ask if Tootie is there, and you sort of stay behind me as if you had just come along for company."

"I know," said Rosemary. "I wouldn't want to spoil the Amy's fun by not being surprised." The girls turned the corner onto the Bodgers' street. "I suppose Mrs. Bodger's Secret Pal will do something cute, like leaving her a present in some unexpected place." At the first of the year each member of the club drew the name of another Amy who was to be her Secret Pal. All through the year the Amy's surprised one another with anonymous cards and gifts, and at the annual Christmas party the Pals revealed their identities. Barbara and Rosemary had long poked fun at Secret Pals.

Barbara giggled. "And I suppose they'll bring out your presents in the big black umbrella they always use for showers."

"And eat rich, gooey cake and talk about their diets," added Rosemary. "Good old Amys."

"Rosemary, promise me you'll never be an Amy when you get married," said Barbara.

"I promise," said Rosemary solemnly.

Barbara had an uncomfortable thought. "What will I do if Tootie really is there?"

"If Tootie is willing to see you in front of all the Amys, you will know it is true love." Rosemary was obviously amused.

Barbara groaned.

"What's wrong with Tootie?" asked Rosemary. "I think he's nice. A little gangly, but the type that is sure to mature into something. If you'd take the trouble to really look at Tootie you'd see that he's a good-looking boy."

"Nothing is wrong with Tootie," answered Barbara. "He just likes me more than I like him. He's like a big puppy, only he needs to be cheered up all the time."

"Ah," said Rosemary knowingly. "You don't like him, because he makes you feel guilty. You feel you should like him more than you do."

Barbara considered this. "You know, I believe you're right," she said at last. How wise Rosemary had become since she had roomed with a psychology major.

"Every girl has a Tootie Bodger in her life," said Rosemary, "and I suppose every boy has a girl who likes him more than he likes her."

Barbara thought guiltily of Bill Cunningham and then felt even more guilty for feeling guilty. Bill liked her. He didn't give any other girl rides home on his Vespa. Instantly this thought was answered by another. No other girl fed Bill so well.

The girls were silent as they climbed the steps to the Bodgers' house, Barbara phrasing the sentence she would utter when the door opened, Rosemary preparing to be surprised.

"Is Tootie home?" Barbara asked dutifully of Mrs. Bodger when she opened the door. She sincerely hoped he was not.

"Why, it's Barbara MacLane! And Rosemary!" Mrs. Bodger successfully feigned surprise. "Come on in, girls."

"Surprise! Surprise!" chorused the Amys. "Here comes the bride," someone sang.

"Why—it's the Amys!" Rosemary feigned even greater surprise. "I had no idea—Barbara, why didn't you tell me?"

"I was sworn to secrecy," said Barbara, admiring her sister's performance as she faced the room full of her mother's friends. Although the sisters had always lumped the Amys together, there was actually a vari-

ety of women in the room—the Amy who wore leather
sandals and wove her own skirts, another who was ac-
tive in the League of Women Voters, the mother
whose calm was never disturbed by her six children, a
mother who wanted to write but could not find time,
an Amy whose rough hands and deep tan were the
result of hours spent in her hillside garden.

"And there's Aunt Josie! And Gramma!" exclaimed
Rosemary, surprised, radiant, and bewildered all at
once. "Mother, how ever did you manage not to
breathe a word of this?"

As Mrs. Bodger took the girls' coats Barbara observed that her mother had been right. Tootie was nowhere in sight. She felt her aunt's tape-measure eye
slide over her, making her wish she had not eaten so
many brownies and pecan crispies. Quickly sitting
down on the floor with some of the younger Amys,
she counted the house and prepared to enjoy herself.
Twenty-eight, not counting Rosemary. A lot of loot.
She leaned back and waited for Mrs. Bodger to drag
out the big black cotton umbrella loaded with gifts.

"What a beautiful ring!" cried one of the Amys, and
Rosemary, in answer to the clamor, held out her left
hand as if she dripped jewels from every fingertip.

"Oh no, Mrs. Baylis, let me sit on the floor," said
Rosemary to one of the Amys who was offering her
the seat of honor after everyone had admired her engagement ring. She sank gracefully to the floor near
her grandmother's feet. She smiled around the room at
the members of the club and managed not to look ex-
pectant. Barbara admired her for this ability. If Barbara were the bride, she would probably be looking
down the hall watching for the presents to be brought
on. Mrs. Bodger sat as composed as if there were to
be no presents.

"Rosemary, tell us about your young man," someone

was saying, when the conversation was interrupted by the sound of an alarm clock ringing nearby.

"That is for you, Rosemary," said Mrs. Bodger. "Find the clock, and you will find your first present."

What a typically Amy idea, thought Barbara, controlling her desire to giggle.

All the Amys laughed and Rosemary right along with them. She was a picture of pretty confusion as she stood up and looked in the direction of the sound. She located the clock and the gift behind some books in the bookcase and pulled them out. "Oh—how do I turn this thing off?" She examined the chattering clock in her hand.

"Push the thing on top to the right," directed the clock's owner.

The clock silenced, Rosemary sat down on the floor to open the gift. She read the card, exclaimed over the wrapping, couldn't bear to untie the bow—it was so beautiful—accepted a pair of scissors from her hostess, and finally lifted the lid from the box and laid back the tissue paper, revealing a set of linen dish towels printed with herbs, fruits, and vegetables. Through all this, her ring hovered and sparkled and twinkled like Tinker Bell. Never, it seemed to Barbara, had a left hand been so conspicuous.

"Oh, thank you, Mrs. Lessing," said Rosemary. "They are lovely. And how did you ever know I don't have a single dish towel?" She had lifted each towel out of the box to admire it and then laid them back to pass around the room for all the Amys to examine. By the time she had done this a second alarm clock jangled, this time from a bedroom.

"Another?" You would think Rosemary had not expected a second gift.

When the second clock was located and silenced, Rosemary returned to the room with a large box, wrapped in paper printed with wedding cakes. "I can't imagine what could be in such a big package," she said, and once more read the card. "Why, it's from Mrs. Carretta!"

Barbara began to wonder how her sister was going to manage to be surprised twenty-eight times in one evening. This gift turned out to be a big cooky jar in the shape of a fat and smiling chef. It was the sort of thing Rosemary did not like, but she removed the head with her left hand and peeked inside, exclaiming, "It's going to keep me busy filling this up for Greg. Thank you, Mrs. Carretta." Anyone would think Rosemary had been hoping someone would give her a cooky jar exactly like this.

Clocks continued to buzz, clatter, and jangle at regular intervals. The pile of gifts and ticking clocks beside Rosemary grew. "If this keeps up, she'll get the big head before the wedding is over," Gramma was heard to remark to the Amy sitting next to her. Rosemary pretended not to hear and continued to be surprised and delighted. Barbara genuinely admired her sister's performance, all the more so because her own face was beginning to feel a little stiff from smiling and exclaiming and admiring so much. Pumpkin-colored towels, a casserole, a set of canisters, a wooden salad bowl, two aprons. . . .

One alarm clock produced two gifts. The first was a recipe file, containing the favorite recipe of each Amy. "Why, this one isn't for me," said Rosemary, as she picked up the second gift and read the card, "To Nancy Bodger, my Secret Pal. She is really quite a gal."

"For me?" explained Mrs. Bodger, taking the gift and examining the card. "I can't imagine who it's from. I don't recognize the printing."

Barbara could hardly keep from giggling. The Amys were always rhyming gal and pal. She sought her sister's eye to exchange a private look that would say, How like the Amys! But the smiling eyes of Rosemary refused to be caught. She was much too busy looking at the recipe file she had just received. "I can't wait to try all these recipes," she was saying. Barbara felt lonely and left out. She smothered a yawn.

"Thank you, Secret Pal, whoever you are," said Mrs. Bodger, when she opened her gift, a pair of sequin-trimmed pot holders. "Just what I've always wanted."

As Rosemary's pile of gifts and ticking clocks continued to grow, Barbara found it more and more difficult to smile. A cookbook, more linen dish towels, a set of pink bathroom towels with elaborate hand-crocheted borders from Gramma, who said, "I do like to see pretty colors in a bathroom," and Barbara's candlesticks, looking impractical among the practical gifts. "I love them!" cried Rosemary, when she had undone the olive-green paper, and Barbara found it difficult to return her smile. Her legs were beginning to feel cramped from sitting on the floor. Her left foot was asleep.

Barbara was embarrassed when Aunt Josie patted her hand and said loud enough for all to hear, "You just wait. Your turn is coming." Oh, don't mind me, Barbara thought, I'm just the sister of the bride.

The Amys all laughed affectionately, and Barbara smiled with stiff lips. I'm jealous, she thought miserably. Green-eyed over a lot of dish towels. She would feel better, she knew, once she and Rosemary were home behind the closed door of their room, where they could break down with laughter over the Amys. Sequin-studded pot holders from a Secret Pal! How typical and how delicious!

Still the alarm clocks rang and still Rosemary sustained her performance. Her engagement ring sparkled over the growing pile of gifts. Not once did her delight and enthusiasm flag. Barbara shifted her legs from one side to the other, because her right foot was beginning to go to sleep. She struggled to hide her letdown feeling by sitting up straight and trying to look vivacious. The most admired gift of all was Mrs. MacLane's set of stainless-steel mixing bowls. Every one of the Amys, it seemed, had always wanted a set of such bowls. If the recipe called for melted shortening, it could be melted right in the bowl, eliminating one pan to be washed. This confirmed Barbara's feelings that they were all bound to their kitchen stoves. Every last one of them. There was no poetry in their souls. Just recipes.

The last gift, which Rosemary located in the kitchen in the oven, was anonymous. It turned out to be a rolling pin, and Rosemary laughed as heartily at this joke, symbol of a henpecking wife, as if she were a genuine Amy. Barbara managed to laugh, too, taking her cue from Rosemary. Humoring the hostess in her little joke was the polite thing to do. Her real laughter would be shared with Rosemary at home.

The show was over, the club broke up into groups, and Mrs. Bodger produced cookies, coffee, and ice cream molded in the shape of wedding bells. As Barbara had anticipated, several Amys protested, "There goes my diet!" The ice cream had been molded so hard to make it hold its shape that it was impossible to cut it with a spoon, so the Amys chatted while they chipped away at their wedding bells, waiting for them to soften. Barbara found herself listening to stray bits of conversation that flew about the room. She learned that Mrs. Ellowitz's daughter, who had gone East to college, felt that her mother used too many dashes in her letters. The Amys thought this was extremely funny and agreed that it must be difficult to write to a daughter who had become a literary critic during her first year in college. She learned that Mrs. Baylis's son had had a difficult time selecting a birthday gift for his girl—nothing his mother suggested was right—but he had finally—thank goodness!—settled on artificial pearls. This was interesting to Barbara, who had not realized that Jim Baylis and Betsy, whom she knew at school, had reached the gift-exchanging stage.

For a moment Barbara wished Bill Cunningham's mother was an Amy. She might have learned something interesting about him—whom he was taking to his graduation party, for example—but of course Mrs. Cunningham would never waste her time with a club like the Amys. She was too busy with her career and too tired from her commute to the city.

Barbara found herself being drawn into one of the groups of mothers, who were obviously being kind because she looked left out.

"Won't Rosemary make a lovely bride?" remarked Mrs. Tolfree to Barbara, but glancing across the room at Rosemary.

"Yes." Barbara could not think of anything to add. Rosemary, surrounded by admiring mothers, looked pretty and radiant, just the way a bride should look. She used the hand that bore her engagement ring as self-consciously as if she were wearing wet nail polish.

"Just lovely," agreed the others. Barbara wondered why she felt so tired. She wanted the party to end, and she was sure no one would say she would make a lovely maid of honor tonight.

"Brides of today are certainly different from those of our generation," remarked Mrs. Tolfree. "I can't think of a single girl, when I was in college, who went on to school after marrying."

"They marry so young nowadays," said another Amy, and it seemed to Barbara she sounded a little sad, as if marrying young was something to be sorry about.

Barbara felt it was time for her to contribute to the

conversation, so she said earnestly, "Rosemary feels that if she didn't go on to school she might not use her mind. Rosemary feels it is important for women to use their minds."

She spoke into one of those sudden silences that fall in any crowd and was quite unprepared for the reaction to her remark. Gramma was first to speak. "Oh, for pity's sake!" she exclaimed, as if exasperated with such nonsense.

Barbara was embarrassed by the laughter of the entire roomful of Amys. Hoping at least for silent support, she glanced at Rosemary and saw that she, too, was embarrassed. Me and my big mouth, thought Barbara miserably. She would never hear the last of this. Once the Amys got hold of something to laugh at they never let it drop. They could keep one wretched little joke alive for months, even years. Now they would be asking her if she was using her mind every time they saw her. She could hear them already. Why, hello, Barbara. Still using your mind?

"Addie, do you ever worry about using your mind?" one Amy asked another.

"Using it!" laughed Addie Smith. "With four children it's all I can do to keep from losing it! Meals to plan, washing to do—why, just the laundry alone. . . ."

She needn't sound as if she bent over a scrubbing board, thought Barbara, her feelings still ruffled by the laughter she had brought forth. She knew perfectly well that Mrs. Smith had both an automatic washer and a dryer.

"The chauffeuring to ballet lessons and dental appointments," continued another mother.

"The P.T.A.," chorused several.

"Brownies and Cub Scouts," someone added.

"But I used to feel exactly the same way as the girls," said one of the members, taking Barbara's side. "When I was first married I conscientiously went to the library once a week and followed a reading list on world affairs. I didn't want to stagnate, just because I was married. Until the children came, that is. After that I didn't have much time for world affairs. I was too busy on the home front."

Thank you, thought Barbara.

"Why, that's right," said someone, remembering. "When the Amys first became a club we used to give book reviews. I remember giving Jan her bottle while Addie reviewed *The Grapes of Wrath*." Jan was now married and had two babies of her own.

Gramma leaned over and patted Rosemary's hand. "May all your troubles be little ones."

The Amys all laughed affectionately at Gramma's old joke and at Rosemary's pretty confusion. Each had her own memory of the early days of the Amys to share with someone, and soon the club had broken up once more into chatting groups. To cover up her embarrassment Barbara passed cookies and helped Mrs. Bodger carry plates and coffee cups into the kitchen. She felt somewhat better when she overheard an Amy murmur, "The MacLane girls are both lovely girls." But her pleasure was immediately tempered when the woman added, "Their mother has done such a good job on them." Barbara did not like to think of herself and her sister as a job her mother had done, as if she and Rosemary were pieces of silver to be polished.

Barbara was glad when the party was finally over and they could say good-by to the Amys and carry Rosemary's gifts out to the car. She rode in the back-seat beside the gifts with a casserole on her lap.

"It was a nice party, wasn't it?" remarked Mrs. Mac-Lane, as she backed the car around and headed toward home.

"Just lovely," agreed Rosemary.

"Marvelous loot," was Barbara's comment. She was

looking forward to talking over the party with Rosemary when their mother was not present. She and
Rosemary always talked over parties while Rosemary
put up her hair, a custom she was going to miss when
Rosemary was married.

The only place in the MacLanes' crowded house to
store the gifts was in the corner of Barbara and
Rosemary's room, and when all the boxes were neatly
stacked on the floor and the door was shut, Barbara
flopped on her bed and kicked off her shoes. "You
said there would be a present from Mrs. Bodger's Secret Pal," she crowed.

Rosemary smiled but said nothing as she pulled off
her dress and slipped into her robe.

"And wouldn't you just know the Amys would think
up something like hiding alarm clocks with all the
presents?"

"Oh, I don't know," murmured Rosemary, as she sat
down at her desk. "I thought the whole thing was
sweet myself."

Barbara sat up and stared at her sister. "Did you
even think it was sweet when they talked about their
diets?" she asked incredulously. "All that talk about
no starches and Metrecal for lunch."

"Some of them do have to watch their weight,"
Rosemary pointed out. "Lots of people do in middle
age."

Well. This was a surprise. Barbara was both disappointed and hurt. Her sister had gone over to the enemy camp . . . well, not the enemy camp exactly.
Mothers weren't enemies. She was a . . . traitor to
her own generation. No, traitor wasn't the right word
either. Barbara wondered why such warlike words
came to mind when she thought about the friction between the generations. "You'd better look out," she
said, "or you'll turn into an Amy yourself someday.

You'll go around laughing at your children and talking about diets. You might even have a Secret Pal who gives you pot holders trimmed with sequins."

"I doubt it," said Rosemary as she opened her notebook, "but next semester I think I'll join the Dames."

"And what are the Dames?" demanded Barbara, beginning to undress.

"A club for wives of students," answered Rosemary.

"What do they do?" Barbara was always curious about university life.

"Oh—things like having someone talk on nutrition and how to get the most out of the food dollar," said Rosemary.

At least this was on a higher plane than the Amys, who were inclined to exchange cooky recipes. It was evidence that the Dames used their minds.

"And at the end of each semester there is a party," continued Rosemary with a mischievous smile. "That is when the girls who work while their husbands go to school are awarded their Ph.T. degree."

Barbara had heard of a Ph.D. degree, but never of a Ph.T. This was a new one. "What does that stand for?" she asked, pulling on her nightgown.

"Putting Hubby Through," answered Rosemary, laughing.

Barbara groaned. "They sound every bit as bad as the Amys. Worse even."

"Maybe," agreed Rosemary, "but they have fun." She thought a moment before she said, "And so do the Amys."

Barbara slipped into bed and snapped off her light. "You just wait," she said darkly. "Someday you will have a Secret Pal."

"It might even be fun," said Rosemary calmly from the circle of light cast by her study lamp. "And in the meantime I will use my mind by applying it to Plato."

She, too, might have been making fun of Barbara's remark, even though it had been hers to begin with.

"You're not going to study," protested Barbara
incredulously, "not after a party!"

"Far, far into the night," answered Rosemary, reaching for a roller for her hair. Since she had gone away
to college, she had learned to put up her hair while
reading. It was a great timesaver.

Barbara closed her eyes and pretended to be asleep,
but for a long time she lay awake, engulfed in a new
feeling of loneliness. She was losing Rosemary, and it
hurt. She was going to miss poking fun at her mother's
club; she was going to miss talking over parties. She
already missed sharing the same instant understanding of a situation. . . . She missed a lot and was
going to miss a lot more. . . . But Rosemary was
right about one thing. It had been sweet of the Amys
to give the shower . . . alarm clocks and all.

Chapter Nine

One evening a few days after the shower Rosemary telephoned to say that because Millie did not have much money, she had decided the bridesmaids should make their dresses for the wedding. This meant Mrs. MacLane and Barbara would have to make the maid-of-honor dress. The patterns and material had been chosen and Rosemary, in a burst of efficiency, had bought Barbara's material and was having the store send it to Bayview. It was sea-spray-green organza.

Barbara was disappointed at this news. She had pictured a day of shopping and lunch in San Francisco. And what did she get? A sewing job. Mrs. MacLane, although she was glad to save money, was even more disappointed. She could not imagine when they would find time to make a dress, particularly a dress of organza, which was so slippery to work with. Rosemary seemed to think she was the only member of the family who had anything to do. Perhaps it was natural for a bride to become self-centered with all the attention showered on her, but . . .

The second bit of news that affected Barbara was even more of a disappointment. Greg had chosen his brother Bob, a pre-medical student, to be his best man, which was what Barbara had expected, but the two ushers he chose were both married. This sharply reduced the eligible-man-per-bridesmaid ratio and would, Barbara felt, spoil some of the fun. Oh well.

She still had—sort of—Bill Cunningham, even if, in the press of wedding preparations, she was reduced to buying a bag of cookies at the bakery.

"Now, Barbara, you mustn't be disappointed," said Mrs. MacLane, when Barbara had expressed her feelings about ushers with wives. "It is Rosemary's wedding, you know."

"I know," agreed Barbara. "But weddings are supposed to be fun."

Mrs. MacLane looked amused. "There's no reason why you can't have fun."

"Oh, Mother, you know what I mean," answered Barbara. "A lot of old married men—"

"I'm afraid I do know what you mean." Mrs. MacLane looked even more amused. "You were counting on falling in love with someone in the wedding party."

Barbara did not answer. Her mother need not have put it so directly. Besides, it was not true. She had Bill Cunningham, didn't she? Well, didn't she?

One evening Aunt Josie came over with a copy of *Vogue* to show Mrs. MacLane a picture of a wedding gown. It was a linen dress, worn with a lace veil. Wouldn't it look smart on Rosemary? Barbara studied the picture without enthusiasm. A bride should not look smart. She should look beautiful and romantic. While the two women were discussing wedding dresses, Gordy slouched into the room and leaned against the doorjamb, his arms folded, listening without expression to this feminine conversation. He did not say anything. He just listened, bringing the conversation to a standstill.

"Did you want something, Gordy?" asked Mrs. Mac-Lane.

"I was just thinking," said Gordy. "Don't people have music at wedding receptions?"

"Why yes, Gordy, sometimes they do," answered his mother. "People who can afford it."

"My trio would play for free," volunteered Gordy. "Just to get experience. It wouldn't cost a cent."

"Oh no!" Barbara burst out without thinking. "That wouldn't do at all."

Gordy turned on his sister. "Why not?" he demanded belligerently. "We're getting good."

"Now, Gordy," soothed Mrs. MacLane. "What Barbara means—"

Gordy interrupted. "I know what she means. She means—"

It was Barbara's turn to interrupt. "What I mean is, nobody has folk singing at weddings. I didn't mean that you weren't good." She was anxious to soothe Gordy's feelings if she possibly could. She knew he had not forgotten that kiss on the front steps.

"Why not?" demanded Gordy. "I bet Rosemary would like folk songs at her wedding. She's so modern and all. They have folk singers over at the University all the time."

This was exactly what Barbara was afraid of. Rosemary, with her do-it-yourself, let's-keep-to-fundamentals approach to her wedding, might approve of folk singing at the reception.

Mrs. MacLane exchanged a glance with her sister. This was a difficult situation, calling for tact on everyone's part.

Barbara decided to try the reasonable approach. "But, Gordy, you just can't sing songs about having twenty-nine links of chain around your leg or about a frog going courting. Not at a wedding. People would laugh, and you don't want to be laughed at. At wedding receptions people have things like a string quartet playing selections from *Rosemarie*. It says so in the wedding book."

"*Rosemarie!*" Gordy was contemptuous. "Anyway, it isn't your wedding. You keep out of this."

"What Barbara means," persisted Mrs. MacLane, "is

that folk songs are not exactly appropriate to a wedding. So many of them are sad, and a wedding is a happy occasion."

Gordy was more willing to listen to his mother than to his sister. "We could learn some happy songs," he said hopefully.

Barbara wondered about Gordy's idea of a happy song. *She'll Be Comin' Round the Mountain?* *Old MacDonald Had a Farm?* Probably. The Boy-Scout-camp type of thing, like *The Man on the Flying Trapeze.* The picture of the trio, Tim with his horn-rimmed glasses, Al with his blotchy complexion, and Gordy with his hair uncombed, singing at a wedding reception, was so incongruous it was hilarious—or would be, if the wedding was to be in someone else's family.

"No, Gordy," said his mother gently. "This is a small wedding, and I really don't think a trio would be appropriate. Music is used only at large wedding receptions."

Gordy was not willing to give up. "You *are* sending out an awful lot of invitations," he pointed out.

"A lot of them go to people in the East who won't be coming to the wedding," said Mrs. MacLane patiently.

Gordy seemed to slump. "O.K.," he said. "I just thought I'd ask." He slouched out of the room, while his mother looked after him with a worried frown. "Poor Gordy," she murmured when he had gone.

In spite of the wedding the activities of the rest of the MacLane family continued. Mr. MacLane came home later and with more printer's ink on his shirts than usual, because his classes were printing the school yearbook. Mrs. MacLane struggled with lesson plans for her poor students. Gordy, morose since his trio was not permitted to play at the wedding reception, spent his time after school collecting folk songs at the public library.

Barbara was working on a junior-class committee, which was responsible for putting on a banquet for the seniors. She divided her time between the committee and her bridesmaid dress, which she was eager to finish before Saturday. She hoped to go to San Francisco with her mother to meet Rosemary and shop for the wedding dress that she, too, would wear someday.

One afternoon, when Barbara returned home after arguing about decorations with the banquet committee, she found that she had forgotten to shut her bedroom door before she left for school and that Buster was asleep on her bed in the midst of her family of stuffed animals. Pooh Bear, she was sure, had another rent on his fat stomach from the cat's claws. "Oh, you!" Barbara muttered, flinging her books on the bed.

Startled, Buster opened his eyes and glared evilly at her. Barbara snatched him from the bed. "You get out of my room and stay out!" She tossed the Siamese into the hall where, not quite awake, he blinked at her. "Scat, scram, shoo!" she said, and clapped her hands at him.

Gordy, barefoot and wearing a pair of old jeans torn off at the knee, appeared in the door of his room. Barbara had not known he was home. "You leave my cat alone," he said, picking up Buster and petting his dark head.

"You keep your cat out of my room," she retorted.

"Why should I?"

"Because he tore another hole in Pooh Bear, that's why!" Barbara seized her bear and showed it to Gordy. "See!" she said indignantly.

"Aw, grow up." Gordy did not bother to look at Pooh's most recent wound.

This stung Barbara, because it was so close to her feelings about herself. She should grow up. Now that Rosemary was old enough to get married and she soon would be, she had begun to feel that her animals were childish. They were childish and they were *things* that should be put away, but somehow she never found time to do this. "Don't you tell me to grow up," she retorted. "Don't forget I am three years older than you are." She should grow up in her relation to Gordy, too. She was tired of their childish bickering. She wanted to stop, but she could not bring herself to give in and be the first to declare a truce.

"Yeah, old enough to smooch on the front steps with old Bill Cunningham," said Gordy. Her remarks about his playing at the wedding reception had not helped his feeling toward her.

"We weren't smooching," cried Barbara. "I wish you wouldn't use that word."

"When is he going to stop stuffing himself with our cookies and take you out?" asked Gordy.

This stung even more, because Barbara had been wondering the same thing. Until now she had persuaded herself that her family had not noticed this omission on Bill's part. She had been sure her family thought she and Bill were just good friends—pals, buddies, that sort of thing. "Don't worry. He will," she prophesied, and sincerely hoped her prophecy would come true. She had a lot of cookies invested in Bill.

"Ha!" said Gordy darkly. "That'll be the day." Even Buster, draped over Gordy's arm as if he had no bones, seemed to leer at Barbara.

"Oh, keep quiet!" Somewhere—Barbara was not sure at exactly what point—she had lost the argument, and she felt humiliated at having to retire in defeat before her brother.

"Why should he take you out when he can hang around eating cookies and smooching on the front steps?" asked Gordy with a grin. He could afford to grin. He had won the argument.

Barbara tried to salvage a few shreds of dignity. "After all, Bill gives me a ride home. The least I can do to repay him is offer him a cooky and some milk."

Gordy merely laughed and retired to his room, where he began to strum his guitar. There was nothing left for Barbara to do but retire to her room also, but she closed her door a little harder than necessary when Gordy began to sing *Careless Love*.

Sadly she picked up Pooh and her stuffed penguin and hugged them while she reflected that Gordy had been irritatingly right about a couple of things that afternoon. She was too old for stuffed animals, and Bill had never even hinted at anything more than a ride home on his Vespa, even though he was about to be graduated from high school and would be going to the all-night party sponsored by the P.T.A.

Barbara began to open dresser drawers until she found one of Rosemary's empty. She appropriated it for her animals, because Rosemary would no longer need it. She hugged each animal and pressed it to her cheek before she laid it away. Then, carried away with the idea of getting rid of nonessential *things*, she cleared her mirror of a clutter of party invitations, dog-eared snapshots, and last year's football pompon, and swept them all into the wastebasket.

Barbara was looking around the room, thinking how uncluttered it looked and how much easier to dust, when she noticed that Gordy was no longer singing to taunt her. He was experimenting with a new song that sounded like *Ten Little Indians*, but the words were different. She sat down on her bed to listen.

"*Unos et duo tres parvi Indi*," sang Gordy, fumbling with chords. "*Quattuor quinque et sex parvi Indi, septem et octo et novem parvi Indici, decem pueri Indici.*" Gordy was singing *Ten Little Indians* in Latin.

"*Unos et duo tres parvi Indi,*" he began again with different chords.

Barbara understood at once that Gordy's trio was going to sing at the junior high school's annual Latin banquet. Their first public appearance. And as angry as Barbara was with her brother, she was also glad for him. He had worked so hard. She sat on the bed remembering her own Latin banquet, always the high point in junior-high-school social life in Bayview. Some students were thought to elect Latin just so they could go to the banquet, wear Roman costumes, and eat lying on the floor.

"*Septem et octo et novem parvi Indici,*" sang Gordy, and this time he played his chords with more assurance.

Remembering, Barbara smiled, and at the same time she got up and opened the drawer of stuffed animals, gave Pooh one last pat on his fat stomach, and closed the drawer again.

As the week wore on, it became evident to Barbara that a homemade bridesmaid dress and ushers with wives were not the only disappointments in store for her. On Wednesday her mother talked to Rosemary and arranged to meet her in San Francisco Saturday morning to shop for a wedding dress and a mother-of-the-bride dress. Although Aunt Josie had offered to buy Rosemary a wedding dress at a discount in the store in which she worked, Rosemary insisted this would not do. She did not want her aunt to choose the dress, and that was how it was sure to work out. Nothing was said about Barbara's going to the city.

"Just think, I will be wearing the same dress someday," remarked Barbara, dropping what she hoped was a tactful hint.

"Maybe," agreed her mother, who was trying to sew her way through a cloud of sea-spray organza on the dining-room table. "But I can't go through another wedding for years. At least ten years."

"Mother!" objected Barbara. "I would be twenty-six."

"Maybe nine years," conceded Mrs. MacLane.

"Oh, Mother!" Barbara was impatient. "I'll be too old by then."

In spare moments during the week Barbara helped her mother make her dress for the wedding. Still nothing was said about Barbara's going to San Francisco. It isn't fair, she told herself. It just was not fair for Rosemary to get to choose a dress that they both would wear. When Saturday morning came and she still had not been included, she gave up hoping and somewhat resentfully accepted her mother's instructions to fix a good lunch for Gordy and for her father, unless he decided to work at school. What a disappointment this day was turning out to be—left to mind the home fires while her mother and sister went off for a day of fun and shopping in the city. She felt like Cinderella, left behind while the wicked stepsisters went to the ball.

"Mother, *please* don't buy any dowdy old lace for your mother-of-the-bride dress," Barbara said, as her mother was leaving.

Mrs. MacLane laughed. "I'll let Rosemary wear the lace in the family. And don't worry. She will be there to keep me from buying the wrong thing."

With her mother and father away, Barbara had nothing to do but hem her dress and feel forlorn. She wished she was in the city helping select the family wedding gown. She loved San Francisco. The flower stands . . . the cable cars . . . the pigeons wheeling over Union Square . . . the air of excitement. Missing a trip to the city for any reason was disappointing, but to have to stay home and prepare Gordy's lunch when she could be shopping for her own—and Rosemary's— wedding gown was almost too much to bear. Rosemary always had all the fun.

Naturally Barbara took her feelings out on Gordy. She put Buster out the back door in such a way that Gordy was sure to hear. Buster sat outside the door and cursed in Siamese. Gordy let his cat in just as noisily as Barbara had let him out. He draped Buster, who went limp and boneless, around his neck like a fur piece and went off to his room to sing, *"Te canno patria, candida libera." America* in Latin.

By lunch time Barbara had hemmed the dress, but in her Cinderella-in-the-ashes mood her attitude toward her brother had not softened. Her father was working, so she made Gordy two peanut-butter sandwiches, which she laid on a plate along with one dill pickle. It was a stark but filling lunch. She left it on the counter in the kitchen and took her own sandwich out to the patio to eat while she wondered if her mother and Rosemary had found a wedding dress that could be worn with a lace jacket, and if Rosemary was making certain that the mother of the bride would not be dowdy.

Barbara spent a fidgety afternoon waiting for her mother to return. She pressed her dress, and when it was hanging in her closet ready for the wedding, she telephoned a friend and talked for almost an hour about school and friends and the wedding. Her friend wished she had a wedding in her family. Barbara ended the conversation when her father came home, put on his green eyeshade, and began to add up bills at his rolltop desk on the sun porch. He and Gordy were at opposite ends of the house, which was exactly where Barbara wanted them since her most recent quarrel with her brother.

Barbara glanced out the window to see if her mother might be coming from the bus stop, but she

was not in sight. She tried to settle down to read a
magazine, but thoughts of the shopping trip she was
missing flitted through her head. Rosemary and her
mother were probably having such a good time they
had forgotten all about her.

Barbara was startled out of her Cinderella mood
when the doorbell rang. Glad for any interruption, she
opened the door and was confronted by two junior-
high-school boys, Tim and Al, the other two thirds of
Gordy's trio, who were dressed in Roman costumes.
They were a startling sight. Al, who was lugging a
bass violin, was a Roman soldier, complete with cloak,
helmet, and wooden sword. Tim was also a soldier,
but he was wearing armor of gold-painted metal over
a tunic. Their mothers must have worked hard. It had
taken hours to sew the braid on those tunics, and
there was a day's work on Al's helmet alone.

Barbara could hardly keep from laughing. They
looked so ridiculous—Al with his horn-rimmed glasses
beneath his helmet, Tim with his blotchy complexion,
and both of them with skinny legs and knobby knees.
But along with her desire to laugh, Barbara was also
touched. They looked so pleased with themselves.
This was to be their first public appearance as a trio.

"Come on in, boys," said Barbara. She called out,
"Gordy! Your trio is here."

Guitar in hand, Gordy came out of his room.

"Gordy!" cried Barbara involuntarily. He, too, was
in costume, a costume he had made himself. It consisted of a sheet draped around him and held in place
with visible safety pins. On his feet he was wearing
zoris, or go-aheads, as they are sometimes called. "You
can't go that way."

Gordy scowled at his sister. "How else am I going
to go?"

"You . . . well, I mean. . . ." Barbara did not
know what to say. Gordy's sheet looked bunchy, and

it was arranged so awkwardly she did not see how he could play his guitar. As for the safety pins—the Romans had a lot of things, roads and aqueducts and coliseums, but she was sure they did not have safety pins. "Why didn't you say you needed a costume?" she asked.

"The whole family knew I was playing at the Latin banquet," Gordy reminded her.

"Yes, but—" Barbara was exasperated. "You could have said something."

"Aw. Everybody was so busy buzzing around about Rosemary's wedding, nobody would have even heard me."

And suddenly Barbara felt sorry for her brother. She understood, because no one seemed to hear her lately either. They were both just the bride's relatives. He had been feeling, just as she had felt that day, shoved aside, neglected. Only it must be worse for a boy. She at least had a part in the wedding, but all he could possibly have was a left-out feeling. He was too young even to be an usher. He had been too proud to ask for help on a costume from a sister he had been bickering with, and no one else in the family had time to help him.

Barbara was ashamed of herself, and with her feelings of shame came the realization that no matter how much she and Gordy quarreled, she cared about his feelings. He was family. They had to stick together. "I'll fix you a costume, Gordy," she offered. There was not much time. She did not know what she could do, but she could try, and the results were bound to be better than Gordy's arrangement of sheets and safety pins. "Get me your Latin book, so I can get some ideas from the pictures."

Gordy eyed her with mistrust.

"Aw, go on, Gordy," urged Al. "You look crummy."

"Sure," agreed Tim. "This is our first engagement.

Nobody will ask us to play anywhere if we don't look good on our first engagement. Anyway, what have you got to lose?"

"Nothing, I guess," admitted Gordy, and went to his room for his Latin book, which he handed to Barbara.

"You go ahead and practice while I look for a fast inspiration." Hurriedly Barbara thumbed through the book, seeking illustrations. From Gordy's room the trio began to sing, "*Unos et duo tres parvi Indi. . . .*" She was surprised at the improvement they had made since the last time she had heard them. They were quite good—for a trio of old Roman folk singers.

If only Barbara had more time. She flipped past a diagram of a Roman house and a picture of gladiators in the arena. She could not turn him into a gladiator on such short notice. Even if he used the garbage can lid for a shield, there was no time to make a helmet and, anyway, he needed his arms free to play the guitar. She examined a picture of three Roman soldiers, a legionary, a centurion, and a Praetorian Guard. No time for those either. It would have to be a toga, after all, but surely she could improve upon what Gordy had created. A picture of Julius Caesar, stabbed, at the foot of a statue of Pompey, was finally her inspiration. Pompey was wearing a wreath of laurel leaves. The MacLanes did not have a laurel bush, but they did have a rhododendron, with similar leaves, growing at the side of the house. She searched the book for a closer picture of a laurel wreath and found one in an illustration of a coin, showing the head of Constantine. The wreath appeared to be tied at the back of the head with a bow of ribbon. Roman hair was different, too. It was combed down over the forehead.

A ribbon. Barbara did not have a ribbon, but she did have a dress with a belt that tied. She snatched the belt from her closet, ran outdoors, and picked a dozen rhododendron leaves. There was no time to try

to sew them to the belt, so she borrowed a stapler
from her father and set to work stapling leaves to the
belt so that they overlapped. It actually worked. The
spines of the leaves were strong enough to hold the
staples.

With the wreath, a comb, and a can of hair spray
she entered Gordy's room. The trio stopped singing.

"What's that for?" Gordy eyed the hair spray suspi-
ciously.

"A genuine Roman hairdo," Barbara told him. "Shut
your eyes." Somewhat to her surprise Gordy obeyed
without argument.

"You sure smell pretty," observed Tim, when Barbara had dampened Gordy's wavy red hair, but neither
he nor Al laughed. This occasion was too important to
them.

Barbara combed Gordy's hair down over his forehead. It was so much longer than Constantine's hair
that she separated it into strands, which she twisted
into flat curls across his forehead. Then she tied the
rhododendron wreath in place and stood back,
pleased with what she had done. But that toga. It
would not do. It was bunched around Gordy's neck.
"Why are you wearing the sheet that way?" she asked.

"To cover up my T-shirt," answered Gordy.

Barbara consulted the Latin book once more. The
Romans who stabbed Caesar appeared to be wearing
collarless, short-sleeved shirts under their togas with
one sleeve showing. "Don't cover it up" she said. "Here.
Do it this way. Throw this end of the sheet over your
left shoulder and let your right sleeve show. See? Like
the picture."

"Sure," agreed Gordy. "But how do I keep it in
place? I need my hands to play my guitar."

"Wait—I'll get a brooch." Barbara found a lapel pin
among her mother's costume jewelry and used it to
anchor Gordy's toga securely to his T-shirt.

"What about his feet?" asked Al, who was wearing sandals and leggings. "From the ankles down he looks as if he was about to go swimming."

What could she do about the zoris? Barbara studied Gordy's feet until she had an inspiration. In the box of sewing things in the closet she found some odds and ends of seam tape. These she tied to Gordy's zoris and crisscrossed around his legs like the ribbons on ballet slippers. She looked critically at the results. "It gives the effect of sandals," she conceded, "and in a costume it's the effect that counts."

"Hail to Gordy, noblest Roman of them all," said Tim, and Barbara could tell that all three boys were pleased with the improvement she had made in Gordy's costume.

"She came, she saw, she conquered," said Al.

"Thanks, Barby," said Gordy. "As Emperor of Rome, I promise not to throw you to the lions."

Barbara looked directly at her brother. "Is that really a promise?" she asked.

"Sure it's a promise." Gordy returned her look. "The Emperor does not go back on his word."

It was as easy as that, thought Barbara. All I had to do was make the first move toward a truce.

"Hey, Dad!" Gordy called out. "You said you'd drive us to the banquet."

"Coming," answered Mr. MacLane from the sun porch.

"Have fun," said Barbara, and meant it. "Don't let anybody stab you in the forum."

Chapter Ten

Several things happened that first week in June, all of
them inevitable, but several of them surprising to Barbara nevertheless. Rosemary's final examinations were
almost over, to the relief of the whole family. Wedding
presents began to arrive, hardly surprising in view of
the shopping bag full of invitations that Barbara had
shoved, a handful at a time, through a slot at the post
office. The University of California announced that it
was raising its standards of admissions, bringing a
new worry into Barbara's life. Scholastically she was
not quite in the upper ten per cent of her class, and
she was no longer sure she would be admitted to the
University.

But the most surprising event of all was Rosemary's
telephone call announcing that she was going to be a
landlady, and wasn't it marvelous? Now she and Greg
did not have to pay rent! They wouldn't have to give
up Greg's car. They might even save money. A couple
they knew—the man had just received his Ph.D.—were
moving out of the apartment house they had been
managing, and when Greg heard about it, he rushed
right over to see the owner before anyone else heard
about it. Now they were going to take care of the
building, collect the rents for the owner, and get their
apartment rent-free. Barbara was not only surprised,
she was a little shocked. Rosemary and Greg would,
of course, have to have a place to live, but somehow

having an apartment to move into made everything seem so final. It was too soon. She did not want time to pass so quickly. As for Rosemary in the role of a landlady—this was too much for Barbara even to try to imagine.

Mrs. MacLane's reaction to the apartment was different. "A very sensible arrangement," she said. "And thank goodness they have a place to live. Now we can take the shower presents over to Berkeley and get them out of the way before we are swamped with wedding presents."

"I'll drive over with them and bring Rosemary and Millie back," volunteered Barbara, who had always wanted to take the car out on the freeways. Millie was to stay with the MacLanes until after the wedding.

"It would be a help," admitted her mother. "I'll talk it over with your father."

Mr. MacLane agreed, but this did not make it easy for Barbara to get away with a carload of shower presents when Saturday came. First she had to listen to her mother's anxious fussing. "Barby, please drive carefully. Remember, driving across the bridge is not like driving around Bayview. And cloverleafs can be confusing if you're not used to them. Cars seem to be coming at you from all directions."

And her father's lecture. "Just remember, an accident will increase our insurance rates, and with a wedding in the family we can't afford one nickel more." And Barbara had her own worries. If she should have an accident she might smash all her sister's shower presents, as well as injure the maid of honor. Yes, she would certainly drive with care.

Barbara quickly settled the matter of clothing for the trip. The thing to do on a trip to a university town was to dress as much like a college girl and as little like a high-school girl as possible. Even though the day was warm she chose a gray-flannel skirt and black blouse Rosemary had left behind. She slipped into her one pair of dark pumps and skipped quickly out of the house before her mother could ask her why she was wearing that warm skirt and her best shoes.

Her parents' warnings fresh in her mind, Barbara drove with extreme care onto the freeway, around the cloverleaf, and over the bridge. Driving this car is my responsibility, she told herself, her mouth dry and her hands clammy on the steering wheel as she kept pace with the fast traffic. When at last Barbara spun around the cloverleaf that took her off the freeway and into Berkeley, she exhaled in relief, and as she drove along the tree-lined streets she allowed her thoughts to fly off to the subject she had been wanting to think about all morning—Rosemary's apartment. Lucky Rosemary, about to set up housekeeping, perhaps in one of the new apartment buildings with a mosaic on the front. Lucky Rosemary, with everything new all at once, everything modern, everything shining, everything color-co-ordinated. Pumpkin-colored towels in the bathroom and linen dish towels, printed with designs of herbs, hanging in the kitchen over the stainless steel sink. All the new pots and pans stored in the cupboards, which would be . . . let's see, what were the magazines showing? Birch. Birch cupboards. Lucky, lucky Rosemary.

Or perhaps the apartment would not be new at all. Probably not. A new apartment might be too expensive. Perhaps it was in one of those brown-shingle houses that had been converted into apartments. It would be old and charming. Barbara could see it quite clearly in her mind as she drove along a street bordering the University, the University to which she hoped to be admitted. The entrance to the apartment was in a garden. The door was painted peacock blue and was shaded by an old redwood tree. The window ledges were wide, and bright with potted geraniums.

Inside, the rooms were paneled in redwood, mellowed to a golden brown. There would be a fireplace, old and quaint, and the furniture would be rattan, with cushions covered in intense colors—greens and blues and violets. The coffee table would be an enormous round brass tray on a stand. The kitchen would be tiny but convenient, built on when the building was converted to apartments. It would have a big window that looked out on a tangle of flowers and shrubs. There would be a fruit tree to blossom in spring. . . .

The blast of a car's horn snapped Barbara back to reality. She concentrated on her driving every second until she came to Stebbins Hall, which would no longer be Rosemary's home at the University.

Barbara felt shy as she entered the front door, and was sure that the men leaning over the Dutch door by the switchboard knew at a glance that she was only in high school. The girls in the halls had such an air of belonging that she felt like an intruder. She made her way around a pile of trunks and walked up the stairs and down the hall to Rosemary's room, where the door stood open. The curtains were down; the blankets were folded on the bare mattresses of the twin beds. It was a box of a room with the two narrow beds, two study tables and chairs, one bookcase, and one dresser. Until Rosemary had decided to get married Barbara had longed to live in a room like this. To share such a room with a roommate instead of a sister, to stay up all night studying if she felt like it, had seemed to her a most desirable way to live.

Rosemary was packing books into a carton, and Millie was washing windows. "Oh, hi," said Rosemary, straightening up. She looked tired. There were circles under her eyes, she had not put her hair up the night before, and she had eaten off most of her lipstick at lunch without taking time to renew it. "My last final was this morning—French. Beginning-language finals always come last, and I was up practically all night cramming," she said, to explain her appearance.

"Hello, Barbara." Millie scraped a speck off the window with her thumbnail. "We can't leave until we wash the windows and the woodwork and scrub the bathroom." Millie's long hair was gathered into a careless knot at the nape of her neck, and Barbara hoped that somehow she could be persuaded to take an interest in her appearance before the wedding. Millie said that girls who fussed a lot about clothes and hair only revealed their feelings of insecurity.

"Anything I can do to help?" asked Barbara, looking out the window Millie was polishing at the row of garages with clotheslines on the roof, where a single forlorn slip dangled, forgotten by some girl in her haste to pack.

It took two trips, past different sets of men leaning over the Dutch door by the switchboard, to load Rosemary's clothes into the car along with the shower presents, and each time Barbara thought uneasily of the higher admission standards. She promised herself she would study much harder during her senior year.

Rosemary and Millie lugged out several cartons and boxes which, they explained, contained canned goods that were shower presents from the girls in the dormitory. Rosemary laughed when she explained that all the cans had had their labels removed. The last thing that Rosemary brought out, carrying it carefully as if it was precious, was a framed reproduction of a picture that Barbara did not understand at all. It was made up of lines and shapes in black, gray, white, and olive green against a terra-cotta background.

"What is it?" Barbara knew it was unsophisticated to ask.

"*Portrait of Moe* by Paul Klee." Rosemary laid the picture carefully on top of her dresses. "A present from the girls in my end of the dormitory. Greg and I think it is terribly good."

If Rosemary said the picture was good, Barbara would try to believe her, because Rosemary had taken a course in art appreciation and must know what she was talking about.

"You go on and help unload your things," said Millie to Rosemary. "I'll finish cleaning our room, and you come back and get me when you're ready."

The moment Barbara had been waiting for, the first glimpse of the apartment, was about to arrive. She drove, following Rosemary's directions, to an apartment house several blocks from the campus. It was a two-story building, old, shabby, and gray, rising from some discouraged shrubbery. It was not at all what Barbara had expected, but she told herself that it would be much nicer inside. Loaded with boxes, the girls climbed the front steps and paused by the row of ten doorbells and names, some typed, some printed, some scribbled. Barbara found a blank space. "Number One. Is this yours?"

"Yes. It didn't seem right to put Mr. and Mrs. Gregory Aldredge on it until we were married. Anyway, I am not expecting callers." Rosemary set the picture by Paul Klee down by the door and hunted through her bag for the key. When she found it she inserted it in the lock, turned it, tried the door, found she had turned it the wrong way, and tried again. This time the door opened, and the girls walked along a dark hall past two strollers that apparently belonged to tenants with small children and past a table that held a dim lamp and a pile of the *Shopping News*. At Number One she struggled with the key once more, and when the door opened she pushed it back and said, "Welcome to our future home."

Barbara stepped inside, and her first thought was that this was hardly a threshold for carrying a bride across. The light was dim, and the air was warm and close, smelling of disinfectant, stale cigarette smoke, and of the many lives that had been lived here. After Rosemary had raised the window shade she remarked, pointing to some cartons in the center of the floor, "I see Greg's been here. Those must be his books and records."

Barbara looked around. The room was small, with a view of the stairwell and the garbage cans of the apartment house next door. The walls were painted the color of dust, and at one end of the room there was a darker rectangle where a former tenant had once hung a picture. The furniture was shabby and of no particular color. There was a large coffee stain on the carpet in front of the lumpy couch. At one end of the room, opposite the dark rectangle, hung a familiar picture of an Indian sitting on a horse. Both the horse and the rider had their heads bowed.

"Did you know the name of that picture is *The End of the Trail?*" asked Rosemary gaily. "Greg and I think it is terribly funny, and so did our friends who just moved out. They left it hanging for laughs." Her fatigue seemed to drop away, now that she had left the dormitory. She leaned the Klee against the couch and stepped back to admire it.

Given her cue, Barbara set her carton of shower presents on the chair. She was astonished that Rosemary could be happy about such a dreary place. In the apartment overhead a small child was pounding the floor with a pan. A melancholy saxophone, startlingly close in the apartment house next door, began to play *Star Dust*. Almost immediately a clarinet in Rosemary's building took up the melody, garnishing it and elaborating on it. The saxophone switched abruptly to *The Old Gray Mare,* and the notes of the clarinet pranced along with it.

"Some jam session," remarked Rosemary. "It goes on every day about this time."

"Somehow I can't think of you and Greg as the landlord and landlady type," Barbara ventured.

Rosemary waved her hand as if it were a wand. "For free rent we will gladly undergo a change of personality. We will probably become a very grim pair, who will pound on the doors at seven o'clock in the morning on the first of the month to demand the rent. Come and see the kitchen."

That kitchen. Its one window looked out on a blank wall next door. The old black gas stove had a high oven. The sink was small and stained with rust. The linoleum was worn and all the cupboards high. Beneath the window was a rickety drop-leaf table, painted light green. The chipped paint showed a stratum of tan beneath the green. The corners of the table and the backs of the chairs, none of which matched, had been decorated by some past tenants with decals of poodles. Another tenant had tried to scrape them off, but had not succeeded. The ceiling was stained where a sink or bathtub had overflowed in the apartment upstairs.

Rosemary opened the door of a small refrigerator, built into the wall beside the sink. "We defrost all the refrigerators in the building from a central switch every Monday night. Can't you just see us madly eating up all the ice cream for dinner every Monday, so it won't get defrosted?" She opened the cupboard doors. "I must remember to get some shelf paper."

Depressed, Barbara stepped back into the living room. She did not like to think of all the new dishes in those dingy cupboards. This was a place where people had come and gone, and that, to Barbara, was the only encouraging thing about it. Her sister surely would not live here long. And the apartment must, at

SISTER OF THE BRIDE · 163

some time during the day, get enough light to fade the wall around a picture that had once hung there.

Rosemary was unaware of Barbara's thoughts and mood. "Come see the bathroom, but don't let it blind you." She opened a door off the tiny front hall and snapped on a light.

Barbara was startled. Someone had tried to brighten the room, which had one small window facing on an air shaft, by painting it yellow. It was yellow all right, bright taxicab yellow. Probably the painter had been surprised at how yellow it had turned out to be. There were cracks in the tile floor, and the wall around the edge of the tub was mildewed. Some past tenant had tried to introduce a note of whimsey over the washbasin with decals of goldfish with flirtatious smiles and sweeping eyelashes.

"Someone must have liked decals," murmured Barbara, wondering how Rosemary would reconcile Klee and flirtatious goldfish in one small apartment.

Rosemary snapped off the light and stepped back into the living room. "Oh yes, a feature I forgot." She pulled a sliding door across the entrance to the kitchen. "See. Greg can study in the kitchen and I can study in the living room and, with a door shut between us, we can't disturb one another."

A bride and groom with a door shut between them. It didn't seem right to Barbara.

"That was the hardest thing about living in a dormitory," Rosemary chattered on. "Having to study in the same room with Millie. She always chewed her hangnails when she had to memorize something."

Barbara was curious to know where Rosemary and Greg were going to sleep, but she did not like to ask. It seemed like such a personal question.

"And now the bedroom," said Rosemary, as if in answer to her sister's thoughts. She swung open a heavy door on one side of the living room. Folded against the back of the door was a bed, the coils of its springs pressing against a blue-and-white-striped mattress. Greg's raincoat was hanging on a hook in the closet behind the bed. "Meet the Murphy bed," said Rosemary. "We'll only have to move the couch two feet every night to get it down."

Barbara was embarrassed to be standing there staring at the lumpy-looking mattress clamped to the springs. She thought of her sister's single bed at home and of her narrow bed in the dormitory, and tried to think of something to say.

Rosemary was oblivious to Barbara's embarrassment. "And since it's out of sight during the daytime, we won't even need a bedspread. That's a saving right there."

Rosemary swung the door shut, flopped down on the couch, looked around at her future home, and said with a happy sigh, "And it's all free for taking care of the yard and the halls, listening to the complaints of the tenants, and collecting the rents."

Barbara wanted to protest, but knew it was not her place to do so. "Isn't it a little—shabby?" she asked mildly, while words like *dingy* and *falling apart* went through her mind. How could Rosemary bring herself to leave her neat room in the dormitory for this?

"That's because it is going to be torn down in a couple of years," explained Rosemary. "The owner isn't doing anything to fix the place up, because the University is going to tear it down to make a parking lot. But long before that, Greg will have his credential and we'll be out of here."

Any time at all in this place seemed like a long time to Barbara. Embarrassed, she looked at the Klee leaning against the end of the couch and found she liked it better now that she was growing accustomed to it. It was interesting to look at, even if she did not understand it.

"And that isn't all," said Rosemary, as happily as if she were pointing out a beautiful view from a window. "The refrigerator is connected to the owner's electric meter and not ours. That's another saving."

Barbara perched on the arm of the one armchair and looked thoughtfully at her sister, resting on the couch in her faded shorts and old shirt. Even to Barbara she looked young, too young to be thinking about rent and the electric bill and having to clean the dreary halls of this run-down building. But there she was, fairly gloating over the owner's having to pay for the electricity to run that little built-in refrigerator, which would defrost every Monday night and melt any ice cream that was not eaten up.

Rosemary sat up. "Let's get to work. At least we can put the canned goods away."

Barbara leaned over and picked up a small can from one of the cartons on the floor. "What do you suppose this is? Tomato sauce maybe?"

"I don't think it would be anything that ordinary," said Rosemary. "The girls said they tried to get things we could never guess. It might be mandarin oranges. People don't buy those every day, and they come in small cans."

Barbara shook the can beside her ear. "It might be chocolate sauce, except it has a wetter sound. Do you think artichoke hearts would sound wet? They are packed in brine or something."

Rosemary laughed. "I don't know. I never listened to an artichoke heart. Or felt its pulse either."

Barbara dropped the can back into the carton. "What are you going to do with all this stuff? Open every can that's the size of whatever you need, hoping you'll find what you want and then ending up with a lot of open cans of things you don't want?"

"We decided to save them for rainy days," explained Rosemary. "If we run out of grocery money before payday, we'll pick out several cans of different sizes, open them and, no matter what they are, have them for dinner."

This was an interesting solution, if not an appetizing one. At that moment there was a tap on the door.

"Our first caller!" Rosemary smoothed her hair with her hands and opened the door.

The visitor was an old lady, straight-backed and sharp-eyed, who was wearing a hat that might have been worn by Paul Revere and carrying an armful of library books. "I'm Miss Cox. Upstairs front," she introduced herself. "Are you the new manager?"

"Yes, I am. Won't you come in?"

"No, thank you. I was on my way to the library when I heard voices and thought I would stop in and tell you that the light bulb in the front entrance has burned out." Barbara, who was watching Miss Cox over Rosemary's shoulder, saw at once that she did not approve of a manager who allowed a burned-out bulb to remain in its socket.

"Oh . . . I didn't know," said Rosemary. "I'll have my . . . uh . . . I'll have Greg replace it today."

"And the garbage was collected this morning," continued Miss Cox. "I thought perhaps you didn't know, since the garbage cans have not been lined with paper yet."

"Why, no, I didn't. Thank you for telling me." Somehow Rosemary was being made to sound guilty. "I . . . I'll take care of it right away."

Barbara was indignant. This was no way to welcome a new neighbor and one who was about to be a bride at that.

"And while I am here I might as well mention those tenants in the rear apartment on the second floor," said Miss Cox. "The ones who let that little boy run up and down the halls all day. He has been leaving his toys on the back stairs, and I very nearly tripped."

"I . . . I'll speak to them," faltered Rosemary, "and I'll take care of the garbage cans right away."

"Good," said Miss Cox crisply. "The former managers were inclined to let things slide."

"What an old biddy!" Barbara burst out, when Rosemary had closed the door and Miss Cox was out of earshot.

"I suppose she has a right to complain," said Rosemary doubtfully. "All the things she mentioned should be taken care of."

"And she will complain, too." Barbara was emphatic. "All the time. I can tell."

"That's what I'm here for, I guess," said Rosemary. "To listen to complaints and not let things slide."

"Oh, joy." Barbara's voice was flat.

"We don't expect to get our rent for nothing. We have to earn it, only I guess I didn't expect to start earning it quite so soon," she reminded her sister with a rueful laugh. "And now—off to the garbage cans!" She tried to sound gay, but her fatigue from her night of cramming had returned.

This was too much for Barbara. A bride should not be lining garbage cans with newspapers. Neither should she have circles under her eyes. "I'll do it," she volunteered.

"But it's my job."

"I'll do it just this once," said Barbara. "To protect your lily-white hands for the wedding. You know. Pale hands I love and that sort of thing."

Rosemary looked at her fingers. "Hands with an inkstain on the forefinger from writing that final."

"Where will I find some newspaper?" asked Barbara.

"In the laundry in the basement," answered Rosemary, giving in. "And thanks awfully."

"Think nothing of it," said Barbara. "I'm maid of

honor, aren't I? And the maid of honor is supposed to
perform little services for the bride, isn't she?"

Rosemary laughed. "I don't think lining garbage
cans was exactly what the author of the wedding book
had in mind."

And neither did I, thought Barbara, as she found
her way to the laundry and snatched up an armful of
old newspapers.

Her thoughts were tumbling about like laundry in a
washing machine. She was shocked by the dingy
apartment, bewildered by Rosemary's happiness over
such a place. Couldn't she *see?* Couldn't she see that it
was small and ugly and shabby and uncomfortable?
That mildew in the bathroom, that awful Murphy bed
standing on its head in the closet. . . . See? Couldn't
she smell? Didn't she know it smelled of meals cooked
and cigarettes smoked long ago? Maybe the old saying was right. Maybe love did blind people. Maybe it
dulled their sense of smell, too. And their sense of
hearing. Maybe, because she was in love, Rosemary
didn't even hear the child banging on the floor with a
pan. How was she going to study with that going on?

There were four garbage cans, and Barbara grimly
set about lining them with newspaper. Rosemary, gay,
frivolous Rosemary, sitting there gloating on that
shabby couch with the lumpy springs, actually gloating, because the few cents it cost to run a refrigerator
would be on the owner's electric bill instead of her
own. And bragging about how she would clean those
halls to pay the rent! What was the matter with her
anyway? Had the poetry gone out of her soul, too?
Even before the wedding?

By the time Barbara had gone to work on the second garbage can, disappointment turned to rebellion.
She did not want Rosemary's marriage to start this
way. Rosemary was going to be a *bride*. Her life
should be as bright and shining as . . . as a picture

in a magazine in which everything matched, nothing was worn, and everyone was happy.

Barbara held her breath and leaned into the third garbage can. She was sure nothing about Rosemary's new life was right. It was all wrong, every bit of it. Barbara felt more and more rebellious, and there was nothing she could do about it. Rosemary had made her decision. If Barbara had been a little girl, she would have kicked a garbage can to express her feelings. But she was not a little girl. She was sixteen years old and on her way to growing up. She could not stamp her foot and say to Rosemary, "I don't *want* you to live this way." She was too old to kick a garbage can. Instead she slammed all four lids down hard and produced four satisfying clangs, like crashes of cymbals in some discordant piece of music.

"Quiet!" yelled someone from an apartment across the way.

When Barbara returned to the apartment she saw that Rosemary had combed her hair and renewed her lipstick. *The End of the Trail* had been replaced by *Portrait of Moe*. Books brightened the bookcase. The place looked better already. In the kitchen Rosemary had set out two unmatched cheese glasses filled with pink juice. "I shook cans until I found one that sounded good and sloshy, and took a chance that I might find some kind of juice. And it was. Have some," she invited.

Barbara sat down and took a cautious sip. "It's good. What is it?"

Rosemary tasted hers. "I don't know, and I can't think of any pink fruit, except pink grapefruit, and it isn't that."

"I think there's a little pineapple juice in it." Barbara tasted thoughtfully. "Maybe the pink is guava. Guava is pink, isn't it?"

"I don't know," said Rosemary. "We'll just have to call it Brand X."

As the sisters sat in the shabby kitchen sharing a can of strange juice, Barbara studied Rosemary, who was staring, her chin propped on her fist, at the apartment house next door, which Barbara was sure she did not even see. She was lost in some private dream, and whatever it was, it was a happy dream, because her lips were curved in a faint smile. When she spoke, she said without rancor, "It's an awful dump, isn't it?"

Barbara nodded. The disappointment and resentment that had twisted into a hard knot within her began to relax. Love had not blinded Rosemary, after all. Now the emotions that had upset Barbara a short while ago seemed . . . well, young. Not everything about Rosemary's life was wrong. There was Greg. And marriage was not something out of the slick and colorful pages of a magazine. It was not just parties and new clothes and flowers and a wedding veil. It was more than having all your friends envying you and wishing *they* had found the right man and wondering if they ever would. It was a lot of other things, too, like love and trust and living within one's income and, in Rosemary and Greg's case, putting their educations ahead of their immediate comfort. Why, Rosemary was prepared to do all this cheerfully, even gaily, and it had not even occurred to her that she was being brave or self-sacrificing. She was doing it because she loved Greg and had faith in his future.

And for the first time the thought came to Barbara that Greg was lucky to be marrying her sister.

Chapter Eleven

The day after high school was out Barbara suspected that she had a broken heart. The trouble was, so many things kept happening that she could not find time to settle down and think about it and make sure. She knew that Bill Cunningham had graduated from high school the night before. She also knew that the P.T.A. had sponsored an all-night graduation party to keep the graduation class from getting into trouble. And since he had not invited her, had, in fact, not even mentioned the party at all, he must have taken some-one else. That was as far as Barbara had been able to think.

To begin with, now that Millie had moved in for what Mr. MacLane called "the duration" and had ap-propriated Barbara's bed, Barbara was sleeping in a sleeping bag on the floor. She spent a lot of time thinking how stiff she was from the hard floor. She would start to think about Bill and the graduation party, and then she would move a sore muscle and think *ouch* instead.

Millie had also appropriated the dining-room table for sewing on her bridesmaid dress. She had not been able to sew on it before, because, as she explained, she had finals. She was so slow and so deliberate in everything she did that Barbara felt frantic just watching her. At the rate she was going she could not possibly finish the dress in time for the wedding.

Hurry, hurry, Barbara thought every time she looked at Millie. Hurry up and finish it.

Sometimes Millie, who had brought her recorder with her, tootled *Sheep May Safely Graze* when she should have been sewing. When she discovered that Gordy could play the guitar, she insisted they try duets. Unfortunately Gordy only knew folk songs while Millie was struggling with Bach, but with a little practice they worked out a very nice arrangement of *The Old Gray Mare*.

Barbara was also distracted from thoughts of a broken heart by the wedding presents, which were arriving by parcel post, express, United Parcel Service, and in the hands of friends, who were of course invited in and served a cup of tea or coffee. And what presents! They might have been for two entirely different brides. Rosemary's generation sent stainless-steel platters and serving dishes, an album of Joan Baez songs on stereo, teak trays and salad bowls, and a set of shish-kebab skewers. The next generation sent crystal—more than Rosemary could store in her tiny apartment—silver serving dishes that would have to be polished, a double-damask tablecloth and napkins, cake plates, and copper molds.

"You're collecting a lot of *things*, aren't you?" Barbara could not help remarking, as she paused with her arms full of tissue paper and excelsior on her way out to the incinerator.

Rosemary answered with a happy sigh. "But it's such fun to open packages. I adore getting presents. After all that work I did on 'Plato: Teacher and Theorist' it's like a heavenly vacation." She went back to writing thank-you notes. She had vowed she would acknowledge all her gifts before the wedding, because after the ceremony she would be going to summer session and would have to study.

Barbara thought this resolution admirable, but she

could not help feeling a little amused at the way marriage was changing Rosemary even before she had taken her vows. She could remember when her sister had to be prodded into writing thank-you notes for her high-school graduation presents.

"That's one thing a college education does for you," explained Mrs. MacLane. "It teaches organization."

"I guess we're getting ready for the countdown," was Gordy's observation about the whole thing.

"I'm not being launched," Rosemary objected, as Greg arrived to take her over to Woodmont for a conference with the minister.

"Oh yes, you are," contradicted her father.

When Barbara was set to polishing silver and had the kitchen to herself, she was at last alone with her own feelings instead of Rosemary's. She unscrewed the lid of the silver-polish jar and wondered about the state of her heart. Bill . . . she thought gingerly. Yes, it hurt even to think about Bill Cunningham. This must mean her heart was really broken because Bill had taken some other girl to the all-night party, had danced till dawn, and then eaten ham and scrambled eggs, served by the mothers of the P.T.A. Now, early in the afternoon, he was probably home in bed asleep. Heartless, fickle Bill. All those cookies, all that milk had been for nothing.

Barbara rubbed polish into the bowl of a spoon with a piece of old flannel. Bill . . . ouch! A broken heart was a sensitive thing. And how sad in the midst of Rosemary's happiness. What a contrast. The hurt was sharp when Barbara thought of Bill as he had been the day before. He had given her a ride home from school, eaten three butterscotch bars and, with a jaunty wave, had ridden off on his Vespa without one word about seeing her during summer vacation. And in September he would be going across the bay to the University. Perhaps she would never see him again, although common sense told her that in a town the size of Bayview this was not likely.

In the spirit of things Gordy sang from his room, "What will the wedding supper be? Ah-hah. Three green beans and a black-eyed pea. Ah-hah." He had been much more agreeable since his trio had been so well received at the Latin banquet, and Barbara was surprised at the improvement in his guitar playing.

Mrs. Maclane, coming into the kitchen, paused to look back at Millie, who was cutting out the taffeta slip for her bridesmaid dress, and Barbara followed her mother's worried glance. Deliberate Millie, wearing a muumuu and beaded Indian moccasins, had laid her pattern exactly on the straight of the goods. Meticulously she had inserted each pin exactly three inches from the last pin.

Now Mrs. MacLane stepped into the kitchen and closed the door behind her. She shook her head. "That girl is driving me out of my mind. She isn't going to finish that dress in time for the wedding if we don't do something drastic," she whispered. "And she spends half her time playing the recorder."

"Do you want me to help?" asked Barbara.

"You'll have to," agreed her mother. "You go on. I'll get Gordy to help with the silver."

Gordy was singing, "Uncle Rat has gone to town. Ah-hah. To buy Miss Mouse a wedding gown. Ah-hah."

"Gordy!" Mrs. MacLane called down the hall. "Come and help polish the silver."

A couple of noisy chords came from the guitar. "Aw, Mom, do I have to?" Gordy wanted to know. "That's woman's work."

"Well, woman's work is never done, so hurry up." Mrs. MacLane's patience was wearing thin.

Barbara found trying to work with Millie exasperating. The dress was finally cut out, but Millie carefully refolded the pattern into its original creases and tucked it into the envelope instead of just stuffing it in, to get it out of the way. She pinned the seams together with pins exactly two inches apart and five eights of an inch from the edge. Barbara, whose own impulse was to sew up the seams on the sewing machine without bothering to baste, could stand it no longer. She did not even offer to help. She simply picked up a needle and thread and started basting with generous stitches. Then she noticed Millie's careful, even stitches, and measured hers accordingly—or tried to. She was too impatient to see the dress finished and too exhilarated, in spite of her broken heart, by the excitement of the wedding preparations to work with Millie's deliberation.

"Aren't you excited that the wedding is almost here?" Barbara finally asked.

Millie licked her finger and knotted her thread. "Not particularly," she said. "I'm not the one who is getting married."

Barbara found this calm infuriating, although she tried to tell herself that it was a good thing. Millie at least would never panic, and there was no telling what the rest of them would do when the wedding day finally came. Barbara loved every ring of the doorbell, every conversation about how many people did they *really* think would stay for the reception, every satin bow, every shred of excelsior. She wished it could go on and on and never end. She dreaded the moment when it would all be over, when the wedding cake was eaten and the rice was thrown and Rosemary had gone off to that awful apartment to live with Greg and be a member of the Dames. She dreaded having the bedroom to herself forever—or until she left home herself.

This brought Barbara back to her daydream of Bill Cunningham. The cooky jar was now empty, the cookies eaten by the bearers of wedding gifts. But it did not matter. Bill was not around to eat them. She hoped Gordy would not notice and make caustic remarks. If he did, she was sure to answer with even more caustic remarks, and that would be the end of the truce they had declared when she had crowned him with the rhododendron wreath before the Latin banquet.

And then unexpectedly Barbara heard the familiar sound of a Vespa in the distance. She had long since learned to distinguish the sound of a Vespa from that of many other motor scooters. She went taut with anticipation. It might not be Bill's scooter, she warned herself, to keep from being hurt if the scooter did not come in her direction. It might not come up the hill. But it did come up the hill. Still she did not relax. It did not have to be Bill's Vespa. His was not the only one in Bayview, she told herself, to stave off disappointment if the scooter passed her house without stopping. But it did not pass by. It really did stop, and Bill Cunningham ran up the steps and rang the doorbell.

"I'll get it," cried Barbara, and sprang up from the welter of silk to hurry to the door before anyone else got there. "Why, Bill!" she exclaimed, as surprised as if she had not heard his Vespa blocks before it reached her house. There were no circles under his eyes. He looked lively and alert, not at all like someone who had danced until dawn. Perhaps he had not even gone to the party. There was nothing for her heart to be broken about, because now she knew Bill really liked her. He had come in the summertime at an hour of the day when he could not possibly be hungry. "Come on in," she said, and smiled up at him.

Bill stepped inside, and Barbara introduced him to

Millie, explaining, "We have been sewing like mad on her bridesmaid dress." And then, lest he think she was too busy sewing to spend any time with him, she added, "I've been basting until my fingers are stiff. I was just going to take a break." She wished Millie was wearing something other than that muumuu and those beaded moccasins, and was glad she felt insecure enough to care more about her appearance. She also wished Millie would go off some place and tootle on her recorder, but Millie did not have this much tact. She said hello to Bill and continued to sew.

"Yeah, I thought you might be sewing," said Bill, and for the first time Barbara noticed he was carrying something rolled up under his arm the way boys carry swimming trunks rolled up in a towel. This was not a towel, so he could not be here to ask her to go swimming. She watched him pull the bundle out from under his arm and unroll it. It was a plaid shirt. "I was wondering—could you sew my shirt? It's my good Viyella shirt, and I tore the pocket. See?"

Automatically Barbara took the shirt and examined it. It was beautiful. The brown-and-green plaid was subtle, the fabric soft. One corner of the pocket had been ripped loose, and the rim of the collar was a bit grubby. Barbara was so disappointed she could have cried. She wanted a date, and he had brought mending. "Couldn't—couldn't your mother do it?" she faltered.

"She doesn't go in much for sewing," explained Bill. "She has this big career and all."

Barbara looked at Bill, standing there so expectantly by the front door, and thought of all the things she had to do before the wedding—Millie's dress to finish, hair to be washed, errands to be run, a thousand things. Maybe she didn't have a career, but she certainly had plenty to do. Suddenly she was mad. Just plain mad. Who did Bill think he was, anyway, eating her cookies day after day and then coming around taking it for granted she would do his mending? She was not his mother. Or his wife. She most emphatically was not his wife. She would not be his wife if he were the last man on earth. His torn shirt was not her responsibility. Just because she fed him cookies did not mean she was going to do his mending. Mend his shirt, and he would be bringing his socks next. Well, she did not want to mend his shirt, and she was not going to mend it.

Barbara looked Bill in the eye. "No, I will not mend your shirt!" she informed him. It was with good reason that Gordy sometimes called her Barbed Wire.

"You don't have to be so ferocious about it." Bill was obviously taken aback. "I just thought—"

Barbara felt ferocious. "I suppose you thought I would be glad to mend your shirt!" she said. "I suppose you thought I would consider it an honor to do your mending."

"Well . . . no, not exactly." Bill put his hand on the doorknob as if preparing to retreat.

"Well, I don't!" Barbara informed him.

Bill stepped back and opened the door.

"And furthermore, it isn't even a clean shirt," Barbara pointed out.

"Well, I'm sorry. You seemed so domestic and all . . . I didn't think. . . ." Bill began to back out the door.

"Obviously you didn't," snapped Barbara. "Well, for your information, I may bake cookies, but I don't take in mending. Or washing." She rolled the shirt up into a ball. "Here. Take your old shirt." She threw it at him with such poor aim that it flew over his head, and Bill, now halfway down the steps, automatically sprang up to catch it, like a fielder cathing a baseball.

"Good-by, Bill Cunningham," said Barbara emphatically. "I don't care if I never see you again."

Bill must have begun to recover from his surprise and to regain his poise, because he said with exaggerated sorrow, "Good-by, dear Barbara, I shall go. It is a far, far better thing that I do than I have ever done before."

"Oh, be quiet!" snapped Barbara and slammed the door. He needn't think he was going to win her over by being funny.

"Why, Barbara," said Mrs. MacLane, coming into the living room with a dustcloth in her hand, "that's no way to treat a boy. You weren't very nice to Bill."

"No, I wasn't," agreed Barbara, "but I don't think he was very nice to me either." As soon as she had shut the door between herself and Bill, she did not know whether to giggle or to cry. The Vespa began to putt off down the hill, taking Bill farther and farther away from her, and to her great surprise a feeling of lightness came over her. She discovered she was tired of baking cookies for that—cooky hound. She was tired of trying to win him, and as for her daydreams about getting married someday, she found them so silly she was embarrassed even thinking about them. Imagine living in an apartment like Rosemary's with Bill Cunningham and washing his socks. Never, never, never!

"I guess you told him," observed Millie, slipping out of her muumuu and pulling on the bodice of her dress to see if it fit.

Barbara had forgotten all about Millie. "Yes, I guess I did," she agreed a bit ruefully, thinking perhaps she had been too hard on Bill. After all, she had led him to believe she was such a . . . a domestic little wren that naturally he would think she would be glad to mend his shirt. Still, she was glad she refused to do it. For the first time she felt that she had behaved honestly with Bill. She only wished she had been a little less ferocious about it, so she would not be left feeling

quite so ridiculous. Oh well, it was all over now. She
picked up her needle and thread and began to baste
once more. That was that. Now to get on with the
wedding.

As Barbara stitched, she reflected that if she did
not learn to get along better with boys, Rosemary's
wedding might very well be the only one in the family. Tootie and Bill. What a pair. But perhaps, as Rosemary had said of Tootie, they might mature into
something, not that she cared if they did. Her
thoughts wandered off into another daydream. Barbara MacLane, career woman. Barbara, a highly paid
writer of advertising copy. Barbara, buried in a laboratory. Barbara, city planner. As the afternoon wore
on, she began to feel ashamed of herself. If she ever
ran into Bill, she would apologize for being so angry.
Not apologize *abjectly,* but apologize nevertheless.

The postman brought another package, and shortly
after that Rosemary and Greg came in, both wearing
the special glow of a couple that has bought a marriage license the day before and has just had a talk
with the minister. Greg refused an invitation to dinner—he was painting the bathroom in the apartment
and wanted to go back to Berkeley—and Rosemary,
smiling absentmindedly, cut the paper tape on the
package with an old butcher knife she had kept handy
since the packages had begun to arrive.

"What is it this time, dear?" asked Mrs. MacLane.

While Greg waited to see the gift, Rosemary opened
the package and pulled out, one piece at a time from a
nest of tissue paper, two sets of silver and salt-and-
pepper shakers.

"How lovely," said Mrs. MacLane. "Doesn't that
make four sets?"

Silver to be polished, thought Barbara. Just what
Rosemary doesn't want.

But Rosemary appeared to admire the salt-and-pepper shakers. "Uncle Charlie and Aunt Ruth," she read from the card. "Mother, promise you won't let Uncle Charlie try to sell Greg a life-insurance policy at the reception."

"Oh, don't mind your relatives," said Mrs. MacLane. "Everybody has them. Your Uncle Charlie can no more keep from selling insurance than he can stop breathing. That's why he's such a good salesman."

"I have a fine collection of relatives myself," said Greg. "I even have a cousin with tattooed ears."

"Really?" asked Rosemary, fascinated.

"A small anchor on each ear lobe," explained Greg. "He had it done while he was in the Navy."

"You never told me that." Rosemary was looking at Greg with love in her eyes, marveling that she had not known he had a cousin with tattooed ears.

"Not an easy thing to bring into the conversation," said Greg.

"And to think that I am going to be related to him," said Rosemary. "What does he have tattooed on his chest?"

Greg laughed. "I don't know. I was afraid to ask." And with that he kissed Rosemary lightly, said good-by to the MacLanes and Millie, and left to return to his brush and paint can in Berkeley.

Soon after Greg had gone and Rosemary was entering the additional pairs of salt-and-pepper shakers in the bride's book, the doorbell rang. "It can't be the mailman," said Rosemary. "He has already been here."

"I'll get it," said Barbara, who was tired of basting on Millie's dress. When she opened the door a delivery boy handed her a long white box from a florist. Without even thinking, she turned it over to Rosemary.

"Flowers? Before the wedding?" Rosemary accepted the box and looked at the name on the card. "But it's for you, Barby."

"Me?" Barbara did not believe it. "Who would send me flowers? I'm just the sister of the bride."

"That's what it says. Barbara MacLane." Rosemary held the box out to her sister.

Still not believing the flowers were for her, Barbara took the box. Sure enough, there was her name on the envelope. "Who on earth?" She tore open the little envelope and pulled out the card. It was not a florist's card. It was a calling card, and it bore the name William Calvert Cunningham. Above the name was written one word—"Regrets." It took a moment for it to register with Barbara that William Calvert Cunningham was Bill Cunningham, who naturally would have calling cards, because he had recently sent out announcements of his graduation from high school. But regrets! Bill Cunningham regrets. Regrets what? That she did not mend his shirt? That she was angry with him? That he had been so thoughtless? She ripped the card in two and tossed it into the fireplace. "That for Bill Cunningham," she fumed. "Let somebody else mend his old shirts."

"Aren't you going to look at the flowers?" asked Rosemary.

Oh yes, the flowers. Barbara lifted the lid from the box and laid back the green tissue paper. Flowers! *One* flower. One single solitary flower, a perfect yellow rose. "Oh, that Bill!" sputtered Barbara, positive now that he was laughing at her. "Of all the nerve." And to think that she had planned to apologize for throwing his shirt at him if she ever happened to run into him again! Apologize! She wouldn't even speak to him. Sending her one yellow rose and his regrets!

"At least it's a rose, not a thistle," Millie pointed out.

"Yes," agreed Mrs. MacLane. "Under the circumstances a thistle might be more appropriate."

"I'd like to send him a thistle," said Barbara darkly. "One dozen thistles."

"Don't be silly," said Millie. "A flower from a boy is a flower from a boy. Look at it that way." That was Millie—practical, down-to-earth, interested and yet detached about other people's problems.

"Yes," agreed Rosemary. "And thank him for the beautiful rose the next time you see him. He'll be surprised." She could afford to be amused by her sister's situation. Rosemary had her man. She was past this sort of thing.

Barbara lifted out the rose and held it to her nose. It was fragrant and perfect, and it was, as Millie had pointed out, a flower from a boy, her first. Perhaps Rosemary was right about thanking Bill. Rosemary had had a lot of experience with boys. She went into the kitchen to find a vase, but none was the right size for a single long-stemmed rose. She finally seized the kitchen shears, chopped the stem in half, and put the rose in a small vase, which she carried back to the living room and set on the coffee table until Buster jumped up to investigate it. Then she moved it to the mantel.

Oh . . . thought Barbara, feeling that the rose was mocking her. Regrets! He is infuriating. She would have moved the rose to some less conspicuous spot, but she refused to attach that much importance to it. It was just a rose. That was all it was. Just a yellow rose. How silly she had been earlier in the day to fancy she had a broken heart. She tested it now to make sure it was all in one piece. Bill. The thought was no longer painful, just infuriating. Resolutely she put Bill out of her mind and got out the ironing board to press seams for Millie.

Barbara put Bill so completely out of her mind that she was entirely unprepared for his telephone call—not that she would have been prepared, even if she had been thinking about him. He had never telephoned her before.

"Hi, Barbara," he said, when she had been called to the phone. "This is Bill. Bill Cunningham."

"Oh. You," she said flatly, because she could not think of anything else to say. He had his nerve calling her after all that had happened that day.

"Yes, me," he said cheerfully. "Still mad?"

"Mad? Why should I be mad?" she asked coldly. Then, remembering Rosemary's advice, she said, "Thank you for the flower. It is very pretty." She did not sound very grateful, but she had not intended to.

Bill, contrary to Rosemary's prophecy, did not seem surprised. "Look, I am sorry about the shirt," he said. "How would you like to go bowling tonight?"

Barbara could remember when this question would have filled her with joy. She could not help reflecting that she was much more mature now at five o'clock than she had been at, say, nine o'clock this morning. "No thank you, Bill," she said politely. "I have to sew on my sister's roommate's bridesmaid dress. We have to finish it in time for the wedding."

"Some other time," said Bill, still cheerfully. "I'll call you."

"Sure, Bill." Barbara made certain her tone carried no meaning at all. Bill did not mean it when he said he would call. She replaced the telephone and made sure the thermostat on the iron was set on "Low" before she flattened the seam on Millie's skirt. She ran the iron over the seam and felt a pang of regret. Now why did I act that way? she asked herself. He had offered an apology; she should have accepted it. She discovered, now that it was too late, that she still liked Bill and that she wanted to go bowling with him. She was not in love with him and did not particularly want to be. She just liked him. She liked his gaiety and his brashness. He was fun, and that, she decided, at her age was a perfectly good reason for wanting to go bowling with a boy.

Oh well, Barbara thought, as she disconnected the iron and carried the skirt back into the dining room. Maybe she had done everything wrong, and it was too late to do anything about it. She could always fall back on Tootie. Good old Tootie. As Rosemary had predicted, he was almost sure to mature into something interesting.

Chapter Twelve

The day before the wedding the MacLanes congratulated themselves that the plans were going smoothly. This was due, Barbara was forced to admit, to help from the Amys rather than to efficiency on the part of the MacLanes, who at this stage were inclined to forget what it was they had started to do. The Amys had many talents. One member, who had once been a dress designer, had designed and made the short veil and jacket from the tattered wedding veil, with scarcely a scrap wasted. The member with a green thumb had volunteered to decorate the church with flowers from her garden. The only Amy who owned a large punch bowl was going to make the punch, and another Amy was giving the rehearsal dinner. Barbara and her mother were most grateful of all to the Amy who dropped in to admire the wedding presents, watched Millie stolidly sewing her way through the sea-spray organza, and simply took the whole thing away from her and that morning had returned it, complete and pressed.

But all this help from the Amys left the MacLanes with little to do, and not having anything to do made them as restless as Buster on a windy day when his fur was full of static electricity. Immediately after lunch the bride, glad for somewhere to go, went off to have her hair done, and when she returned she announced, "I am going to sit up all night, so I won't muss my hair for the wedding." She smiled radiantly, showing her teeth from which the bands had been removed only the day before, solving the problem that had worried Barbara ever since Rosemary had announced she was going to get married.

"You're beginning to look like the singers on TV, who manage to sing and show their teeth at the same time," remarked Barbara.

"Here comes the Bride," sang Rosemary toothily. Then she said, "My mouth feels so wonderfully roomy with just teeth and tongue and no bands."

Shortly after Rosemary returned from the beauty shop Mrs. MacLane and Millie left to have their hair done. Barbara, feeling a little smug, merely washed her naturally curly hair and arranged it with a few flicks of her comb. When she came out of the bathroom she found that Greg had arrived dressed for the rehearsal dinner and was looking at the wedding presents. Barbara saw him pick up a silver vegetable dish three different times, and each time he looked at it as if he had never seen it before.

Rosemary, who had given up writing thank-you notes until after the wedding, was entering gifts in her bride's book. Barbara picked up a copper mold, which she, too, had examined several times—or perhaps she had examined several identical molds. By now there were many duplications among the wedding presents. "Don't you have several of these fish-shaped copper molds?" she asked Rosemary.

"M-hm," answered her sister. "It's all right. They all came from the same shop and are practically legal tender. I can exchange them for something else."

Buster stalked out of Gordy's room and miaowed at the front door. "The cat wants out," said Rosemary, without looking up from her satin-bound book.

"Wants to go out," corrected Greg, speaking absentmindedly as he glanced at his watch. "The cat wants to *go* out."

Rosemary turned and looked up at Greg in surprise. "That's what I said." She looked a little tired, and Barbara hoped she had not been serious about sitting up all night to keep her hair from getting mussed.

"No, you didn't," contradicted Greg. "You said, 'The cat wants out.' You are using an abverb as a predicate objective."

Rosemary raised one eyebrow. "Oh? I am?"

This was ominous. Please, Rosemary, thought Barbara, lower your eyebrow.

"Yes," said Greg, unaware of the emotion indicated by Rosemary's eyebrow. He had a lot to learn about his bride. "That was one of the first things I noticed about people out here. They said they wanted in or they wanted out, when they meant they wanted to come in or they wanted to go out."

The white-satin book was slammed shut. "That's very interesting. No doubt people 'out here,' as you put it, wanted to *go* out or to *come* in to get away from stuffy Easterners like you."

"Perhaps I am being a little stuffy," admitted Greg, but it was too late.

"For your information," said Rosemary, fuming, "I am not a student in English 1A. And it might interest you to know that when I entered Cal I passed my Subject-A examination with flying colors and did not have to take bonehead English. An adverb as a predicate objective, for Pete's sake! How stuffy can you get?"

Rosemary, please, just once let one member of this family suffer in silence, thought Barbara. Don't have a civil war, East against West, bride against groom, just before the wedding.

"O.K., O.K., I admitted I was stuffy. I am sorry.

What more do you want?" Greg scowled. "And for your information, you may have passed your Subject A, but you did not pass with flying colors as you put it. Students either pass or fail. No grades are given."

Buster twitched his tail. Barbara wanted to open the door for him, but Rosemary and Greg had apparently forgotten her, and she did not want to remind them of her presence while they were quarreling. Besides, she wanted to see what happened.

Rosemary, irritated because Greg was right, pursed her lips and entered another present in her bride's book. Buster miaowed again. "The cat still wants out," Rosemary said, with icy emphasis on each syllable.

"Then why don't you let him go out?" Greg's syllables were equally icy.

Barbara was about to open the door for the cat, when Rosemary said, "I shall," and went to the door and opened it. Buster walked out regally, all but his tail. He paused to reconnoiter before allowing the door to be shut behind him. Rosemary gave him a shove with her toe and closed the door unnecessarily hard. "I am interested to learn that you are not only stuffy, you are also inflexible," she said to her fiancé, as she sat down once more to her bride's book.

"I am not inflexible," said Greg, "I am correct."

"I don't know about Eastern cats, but out West the cats want out," Rosemary informed him. She was silent a moment, and then she added in an exaggerated drawl, "Out West we all keep cats that want out, podner. We all speak in the vernacular."

"Now you are being childish as well as ridiculous," said Greg.

"Very interesting." Rosemary closed the book with a bang.

I've got to stop this somehow, Barbara thought desperately. She glanced at her watch. It was after six.

Where were her mother and Millie? "What difference does it make?" she asked at last. "The cat is out."

Both Greg and Rosemary turned on Barbara. "You keep out of this," said Rosemary. "It involves something far more important than the cat, and I am glad I found it out before it was too late."

Barbara hunched her shoulders in embarrassment. What was she supposed to do? Pretend she was deaf? Slink out of the room? She could feel the tension mounting until she could stand it no longer. She rose and said, "I don't know about you, but I am going to dress for the rehearsal dinner. Rehearsal for your wedding. Remember?" With that she left them alone.

That cat, thought Barbara bitterly when she was in her room. She always thought he looked like the spirit of evil, and now she knew this was what he was. He had jinxed the whole wedding. This very minute Rosemary and Greg were probably agreeing the whole thing was a terrible mistake. They were probably deciding to call the wedding off. But *how?* How could they call it off? How could they notify all the people on such short notice?

All those wedding presents that were hard to pack—glassware, the electric mixer, the waffle iron—where would they ever find enough cartons and excelsior to return all those things? And the wedding cake that was probably being baked this very minute. Who would eat it? The family, probably. How ghastly to have to eat their way through the entire cake of a wedding that was called off. It would take at least two weeks. And Millie . . . how awkward to have a stray bridesmaid around the house, but perhaps she could exchange her ticket and leave sooner. And the apartment in Berkeley, already filled with phonograph records and shower presents. Who would move those things out? And that picture by Paul Klee. How could Rosemary return a present that had come from several girls, who had all gone home for the summer? And all those cans without labels. Rosemary could not possibly return those. The MacLanes would probably have to eat them up along with the wedding cake.

Barbara felt like crying as she thought of all those beautiful wedding presents, and she wondered where they would start. Aunt Josie could be called in to help. She could get cartons from the store where she worked. . . . And all those invitations that had gone out. It would be dreadful to let the guests arrive at a cold, empty church, but perhaps the Amys could help. They could organize and telephone everyone. Barbara's heart was flooded with gratitude for the Amys, who could always be counted on to help one another out. Bless them all. No wonder they ate rich desserts. They needed quick energy to keep up with their families' problems.

Barbara was thankful to hear her mother drive up beside the house. She slipped out of her room and out the back door to meet her. "Mother," she whispered, "something terrible has happened. Rosemary and Greg have had an awful quarrel. She said he was stuffy and inflexible, and he said she was ridiculous and childish, and she said she was glad she found it out before it was too late and—oh, it was awful. Mother, what are we going to do?"

Mrs. MacLane began to laugh.

"But, Mother, it's *serious*," protested Barbara.

"Serious or not, it's still funny," said Mrs. MacLane.

"It's probably just wedding jitters," said Millie.

"But, Mother, you should hear them," persisted Barbara, trying to make her mother understand the gravity of the situation. Her mother waved her aside. It was time to dress. She could not be bothered listening to the details of a silly squabble between the bride and groom. All brides and grooms were tired and ner-

vous before the wedding, and Rosema̶
must be especially tired because of the
examinations. But they *would* insist on getting
ried between finals and summer session. . . .

Filled with trepidation, Barbara followed her
mother and Millie into the house. She was shocked at
the glimpse she caught, of Rosemary with the butcher
knife in her hand. "Rosemary!" she cried out.

Rosemary whirled around, the knife still in her
hand. She was smiling. "More presents! Whee!" With
the butcher knife she began to saw at the cord on a
large carton while Greg watched her with amusement.
They no longer looked tired and strained. They looked
positively refreshed.

"But—" began Barbara, and stopped. She decided
she could not keep still. "But you were quarreling just
a few minutes ago. I thought you were going to call
off the wedding."

"Oh, that. Just a lovers' quarrel." Rosemary airily
waved the butcher knife and laughed. "Besides, we
couldn't possibly call off the wedding. How would we
ever get all those wedding presents returned?"

"But to quarrel just before the wedding," persisted
Barbara, baffled by her sister's flippancy. "A wedding is supposed to be perfect."

Rosemary laughed. "How can a wedding be perfect?" she asked. "It involves people. Besides, I don't
mind quarreling. Not when it's so heavenly to make
up." She bestowed upon the groom a dazzling smile,
which he returned with a look filled with love and
amusement.

"My child bride," he teased.

They will have other quarrels, too, just like ordinary
married people, thought Barbara, disillusioned. The
emotions of the afternoon, which seemed to stimulate
the bride and groom, were tiring to Barbara, and she
did not feel that she was at her best when she arrived

at the Lessings' house with her family for the rehearsal dinner. The first person she saw above the other heads when she entered the house was Tootie Bodger.

"Mother," whispered Barbara while they were in the bedroom removing their wraps, "what is Tootie doing here?"

"Angie Lessing felt you wouldn't have any fun unless there was a boy here for you," her mother explained.

Barbara was indignant. "But the best man is mine."

"Only coming out of the church," her mother told her with a smile. "Now be a good sport and be nice to Tootie. There aren't enough men to go around as it is."

"I'm always nice to Tootie," Barbara told her mother. "That's the trouble. I'm nice to him, so he likes me more than I want to be liked."

"These things are like bread and marmalade," said Mrs. MacLane. "They rarely come out even."

Except with Rosemary and Greg, thought Barbara. It comes out even for them. Maybe that was how they knew they were in love. She stepped into the living room to greet the people she knew and to be introduced to those she did not know. Everyone seemed gay and happy, even Mrs. Aldredge, who was now resigned to the simplicity of the whole affair. George and Craig, the ushers, were both attractive, and Barbara could not help feeling it was too bad they were married. Greg's brother Bob was a taller, huskier version of his older brother, and meeting him gave Barbara a feeling of martyrdom—she must renounce this good-looking man for Tootie. Greg's sister Anne was a surprise. Barbara had assumed a Physical-Education major would be a large athletic girl, but Anne was small, with a beautiful figure, a smooth tan, and sleek,

short hair, which was no doubt convenient for swimming.

Barbara kissed her grandmother and her Aunt Josie
and dutifully went to Tootie, who was standing at one
end of the room studying an arrangement of white roses in front of a copper tray as if it was the most interesting bouquet he had ever seen. He had a handful of
nuts and tossed one into his mouth with the regularity
of a metronome. "Hi, Tootie," she said.

"Hi, Barbara." Tootie interrupted his peanut tossing
to smile at her. He looked uncomfortable and uncertain, and Barbara realized that she was feeling the
same way. College students in a group always made
her feel younger than she actually was.

"I don't know what I am doing here," he said. "My
mother said I had to come."

Barbara laughed. "You are here to keep me company," she told him, "and I am not one bit flattered
by your attitude." She looked around the room admiring everyone. Even Millie, in heels instead of those
beaded moccasins and with her hair becomingly arranged, turned out to be almost pretty. Looking up at
Greg's brother Bob, she seemed a different person.
Maybe, thought Barbara, in the midst of all these
strangers she feels insecure enough to care how she
looks.

"Hey, that's swell. I'm glad I'm supposed to keep
you company." Tootie extended the nut dish to Barbara. "Have a nut?"

"Thanks," she said absently, picking out a cashew
nut. She noticed Anne talking to Gramma, and realized that Anne's brother was the only single college
man present. That left Anne without anyone, unless
you counted Gordy, who was a most unwilling guest.
It was nice of Anne to be kind to Gramma. She looked
as if she really enjoyed her conversation with the old

lady, who was a stranger to her. Barbara decided she liked Anne a lot.

"I feel sort of young," Barbara gloomily confided to Tootie. "You know. As if my mother was letting me stay up late because this is a special occasion." Rosemary was flashing a dazzling smile of straight white teeth at everyone. Barbara hoped she would get used to being without her bands before the ceremony. A bride should not walk down the aisle showing off her teeth.

"It's all these college students." Tootie was understanding. "I just tell myself some of them are only a couple of years older than I am."

"All the girls wear eye shadow," observed Barbara. "My mother would just about kill me if I wore eye shadow." She noticed that Aunt Josie and Mrs. Aldredge seemed to be enjoying one another's company, and she wondered if they admired each other's thin figures.

"A girl as pretty as you doesn't need to wear eye shadow," said Tootie.

"Why, thank you." Barbara found herself liking Tootie more than she had realized. It was pleasant to have a boy tell her she was pretty, after weeks of being merely the sister of the bride while Rosemary got all the attention.

"I don't see why girls wear it, anyway," said Tootie. "It looks like gooky stuff to me."

"It is gooky," agreed Barbara. "I tried Rosemary's once." The bits of other people's conversation that she caught seemed so much more sophisticated than this superficial discussion of the gookiness of eye shadow. Talk centered on final examinations at the University of California—the stiff questions asked in Mycology 101, the tricky true-false, multiple-choice examination in Psych 112, the examination in The Novel taken by George's wife, who was saying that the whole examination consisted of just three words: Discuss the novel. How inclusive could a professor get, anyway? She had filled up one and a half blue books answering it.

Mrs. Lessing, the hostess, tried to shoo everyone toward the buffet by reminding them that the wedding party had to leave promptly at a quarter to eight for the rehearsal. Anne graciously served Gramma, so she would not have to get up. Barbara and Tootie moved toward the buffet with the MacLanes and the Aldredges while the college crowd went right on talking about final examinations. "You would think this was a party to celebrate the end of finals instead of the beginning of a marriage," Barbara remarked to Tootie, as they filled their plates and looked around for a place to sit. Tootie solved their problem by pulling a small table from a nest of tables and setting it between two chairs in a corner of the room. They sat down, and Tootie rearranged a slice of turkey that was hanging over the edge of his heaped plate. Voices were rising in the crowded room. Talking seemed an effort to Barbara, who, like Tootie, was hungry. She and Tootie ate in silence while she watched the college crowd gradually move toward the buffet.

"Finals just before my wedding. I nearly died," she heard Rosemary say, "but I'm pretty sure I got a B out of econ."

Barbara, longing to be part of the older group, thought of the newspaper story she had read about the University's raising its entrance requirements, and she despaired. "Are you going to Cal?" she asked Tootie, lifting her voice so that she could be heard.

"I'm going to apply at Stanford, but if I don't get in I'm going to Cal," he answered. "I'm going to major in music, and I'll probably play in the University band and the symphony."

"Are you sure you will get into Cal?" she asked.

"Sure I'm sure. If you meet the requirements the University has to take you. It isn't like a private college," explained Tootie.

Barbara wished she was as assured of her education as Tootie, who had not only chosen his major but his activities as well. It seemed to her that she was the only person in the room tormented by uncertainty. Wistfully she watched the college crowd move toward the buffet. Millie was smiling back over her shoulder at Bob, who was intent on what she was saying. They all seemed so happy and so poised, particularly the two married couples. Just being in the same room with them made Barbara feel as if she were still in mental bobby socks.

"You're not worried about getting into the University, are you?" asked Tootie.

Barbara's mind had wandered since he had last spoken. Unprepared to take up the conversation where they left off, she looked at him, and was surprised to see how interested and concerned he appeared. She also discovered that it was very pleasant to have a boy look at her this way. "I'm sort of worried," admitted Barbara. "I mean, I read this article in the paper that said that fourteen-and-three-tenths per cent of this year's high-school graduates—I think that's what it was—were eligible to go to the University, but that next year only twelve-and-five-tenths per cent—I think—would be eligible. And I just know I'll fall in the middle of the two percentages and won't get in."

Tootie looked sympathetic. "Are you sure?" There was nothing insensitive about Tootie at all. He was a sensitive, understanding boy.

His sympathy was comforting. "I know I'm not quite in the top ten per cent of my class, so I must be someplace in that no man's land between the two percentages."

"How did you do in your preliminary college boards?" he asked.

"All right," she admitted, "but it wasn't my day for geometry. I'll have to do better next spring."

"You could still go to state college if you don't get into the University," Tootie pointed out.

"But I don't want to," Barbara insisted. "I want to go to Cal. Everybody in our family has gone to Cal, and now they have to go and raise the standards just before it is my turn." She nibbled moodily on an olive. "I want to go and, besides, it will be terribly embarrassing if I can't get in. Both my parents being teachers and all."

"And you don't know that you won't get in," Tootie reminded her. "You still have your senior year to bring your grades up in."

By now Barbara was fairly basking in Tootie's concern for her. He seemed so much more attractive than she had ever realized, especially since she had lost Bill, and she wondered if she had ever really looked at him. He had such nice gray eyes that were so understanding it was strange she had never noticed them before. "And I don't know what I want to major in if I do get in," she said. "I read Rosemary's catalogue of courses, and the University has so much to offer, things like criminology and Slavic languages and literatures and religion of ancient Egypt, that I get awed."

"That's one reason for going to the University," said Tootie, "to find out what you want to do. That's why you have to take a variety of courses your first two years."

"I guess you're right." Barbara had heard her parents say the same thing, but somehow she would rather hear it from Tootie.

"Look," said Tootie, "I have this pamphlet on how to study. I got it at the University bookstore when I was visiting the campus once. It sure helped me. Would you like to have it?"

"Oh, yes. I need something like that." Barbara smiled at him across their empty plates and wondered why she had refused to go to the movies with him the one time he had asked her. Perhaps it was his ridiculous nickname that made her feel there was something a little ridiculous about the boy. Well, she had been wrong.

"I'll tell you what I'll do," said Tootie. "I'll stick the pamphlet in your mailbox the next time I pass your house."

Barbara's impulse was to say, Don't do that. Ring the doorbell and come on in. But having hurt Tootie's feelings in the past, she hesitated. Instead she said, "Do you go over to the University often?" and immediately regretted muffing the opportunity that had been open to her.

Tootie nodded. "I go over to concerts quite often. Hertz Hall is small and has good acoustics. It isn't like sitting in the third balcony at the opera house or anything like that."

A date for a concert at the Univerisity would be much more interesting than sitting through a double feature with a bag of popcorn at Bayview's one movie. "That must be fun." Barbara hoped her hint was not too obvious.

Tootie was apparently unaware that her remark was intended as a hint. "I enjoy it. The University offers a lot of good things. They have a good organist, too. I like to hear him play."

"I like organ music," said Barbara, growing bolder.

"You ought to go over and hear their organist sometime," said Tootie.

"I'd like to." Barbara felt she could not possibly make her meaning more clear without coming right out and asking him to take her to a concert, and that she could not do, not after the way she had treated him at school. Before Tootie had a chance to respond to her remark, she was aware of someone standing over them.

It was Greg's mother. Tootie rose awkwardly to his feet. "I've been watching you two young things over here in a corner by yourselves," she said playfully. "Now tell me, what are you being so serious about?"

Barbara did not appreciate being called a young thing, any more than she appreciated the interruption at such a crucial moment, but if Greg did not let his mother bother him, she would try not to be bothered either. "We were discussing the admissions standards of the University of California," she answered gravely.

"Young people are all so serious nowadays," said Mrs. Aldredge, as Mrs. Lessing's cleaning woman, who had been pressed into service for the occasion, removed the plates and set dessert on the little table between Barbara and Tootie. The moment for discussing concerts was gone. Barbara had muffed her opportunity. Tootie had not taken her hint. And what could she expect, she asked herself severely, after all the ducking and dodging she had done to avoid him at school once she had become interested in Bill Cunningham?

Suddenly it was time for the wedding party to leave for the rehearsal. The party at Mrs. Lessing's would continue, but Barbara was sure Tootie would not be there when she returned from the church. First Bill Cunningham and now Tootie Bodger, gone from her life. "Thanks for listening to my troubles," she said to Tootie with a smile as she prepared to leave.

He returned her smile. "That's O.K. I remember how you listened to mine when it seemed as if everybody in the world was trying to make a basketball player out of me."

Barbara wisely refrained from saying, I did? As she

left the party she recalled the how-to-study pamphlet that Tootie was going to put in her mailbox. Naturally the polite thing to do would be to telephone him and thank him for how helpful it was. . . . Or if he did not bring it, she could call him and remind him. . . .

I'm a scheming woman, Barbara told herself happily, and she ran down the steps and climbed into the car beside her father.

Chapter Thirteen

The day of the wedding! The MacLane family awoke early, and Barbara's first thought before she climbed out of her sleeping bag was, Happy is the bride the sun shines on. Except for Gordy, no one felt much like eating breakfast.

"My wedding day." Rosemary looked dreamily out the window while her toast grew cold on her plate.

"Now just relax, dear, and try to eat something," Mrs. MacLane told the bride. "You don't want to be all worn out when four o'clock comes."

"Today is the day I get to give the bride away," remarked Mr. MacLane. "I'll give her away all right. I'll tell Greg she makes terrible coffee and hangs her nylons in the bathroom."

"Oh, Dad!" chided Barbara.

Rosemary merely smiled at her father in an affectionate and absentminded way.

No one seemed able to settle down to anything. An hour or so later the bride said to her mother, "Can't you relax, Mother? Everything is under control. You don't need to flitter about so."

"Am I flirting?" asked Mrs. MacLane, her mind elsewhere. "With six people wanting to take showers before the wedding, perhaps I had better write out a schedule and post it on the bathroom door."

"Me first," cried Rosemary, and twirled around in

the middle of the living room, "because I'm the bride, the bride, the bride!"

More packages arrived, and Rosemary joyfully attacked the wrappings with the butcher knife while Barbara and Millie carted the paper and excelsior out to the incinerator. Another electric blanket, another wooden salad bowl with servers, a silver pitcher. Where would she find room for them all? Greg telephoned, and Rosemary murmured into the mouthpiece, her eyes radiant above the black instrument. No, of course he could not come over. It was bad luck for the groom to see the bride before the ceremony on her wedding day. She could not wait for four o'clock to come.

An Amy arrived with a casserole and a molded salad, so no one would have to think about food before the wedding. Surprisingly everyone was hungry, particularly Rosemary, who had two servings. Barbara did not quite approve of her sister's healthy appetite. A bride's thoughts should be on . . . well, spiritual things.

After lunch the florist's truck arrived with boxes of flowers for the wedding party. "They're beautiful!" cried Barbara, lifting out her nosegay of yellow daisies, each blossom wired primly into place.

"Perfect!" agreed Millie, trying her band of daisies on her hair in front of the mirror in the hall.

"Beautiful!" breathed Rosemary, holding up her bouquet. "And Greg sent white orchids for going away." Then she laughed. "Orchids for the ride back to Berkeley! I adore his sense of humor. I'll put them in our refrigerator and wear them to class on Monday."

Then Mr. and Mrs. Aldredge arrived with Anne, who was carrying her bridesmaid dress on a hanger. Suddenly the bedroom was a flurry of girls and clothes and filled with a rustle of taffeta slips. Disas-

ter threatened when the zipper on Anne's dress stuck,
but Barbara took care of it with a sharp tug. Nothing
must go wrong on Rosemary's wedding day.

"Something old, something new, something borrowed, something blue," chanted Rosemary, as she
pulled a blue-lace garter, the gift of an Amy, into
place. "I need something borrowed."

"That's the wedding veil," said Millie. "It's both old
and borrowed."

"Don't anybody sit down," said Barbara, as she took
her turn at the mirror to adjust her headband of daisies. "The wedding books says we mustn't have wrinkles on the backs of our dresses when we walk down
the aisle."

"How do we ride to church?" asked Millie. "Standing up?"

"Perch on the edge of the car seat with your skirt
hitched up behind you," answered Barbara. "That's
what the book says."

Mrs. MacLane came into the bedroom in her
mother-of-the-bride silk suit with her orchids on her
shoulder. "Girls, you look lovely," she said. "You look
like flowers yourselves. Now hurry along. The Aldredges are waiting to drive the bridesmaids to the
church, and Dad has the car waiting for the bride."

Barbara suddenly did not want to leave her sister or
her mother. "Do I go with the Aldredges?" she asked.

"No, stay with me." Rosemary turned from the mirror to smile at her sister.

"The wedding book says the bride's mother is supposed to leave before the bridesmaids," Barbara
pointed out.

"I can't help what the wedding books says," answered Mrs. MacLane. "This house is just too
crowded."

The bridesmaids were gone, and Barbara was left
alone with her sister and her mother. Rosemary's veil

was pinned in place on her red-gold hair, and her lipstick was modest. She looked as a bride should look—radiant and beautiful. "Isn't it funny? I seem to be the one who is nervous," jittered Barbara, making sure that her band of daisies was secure in her hair. She wondered if she had time to fasten it with one more bobby pin just to be safe.

"Remember, it's my wedding, not yours," Rosemary reminded her.

"I know." There had been moments when she had felt as if it was as much her wedding as Rosemary's, but that feeling had passed.

"Do you have Greg's ring?" asked Rosemary.

"Oh!" Barbara was stricken. She flew to the dresser where the gold band rested in its velvet slot and slipped it on her little finger. She clenched her fist, so the ring could not slide from her hand.

Mrs. MacLane kissed the bride. "You look beautiful, dear, and I'm sure you are going to be very happy," she said. "Come, it's time to go."

"So soon?" Somehow Barbara wanted to postpone the departure a few seconds.

"Let's not keep him waiting at the church," the bride's father called from the front door.

"How do I look, Dad?" Rosemary asked gaily, as she hurried down the hall with her skirts rustling.

Mr. MacLane smiled at his older daughter. "Beautiful," he said gently, and kissed her.

"Gordy. Where's Gordy?" Mrs. MacLane looked around for her son.

"I'm feeding Buster," Gordy answered from the kitchen.

"Well, come *on.*" Mrs. MacLane lowered her voice and shook her head. "Sometimes that boy positively works at being exasperating."

At last the family was going down the front steps.

Barbara was about to shut the door behind her when the telephone rang.

"Let it ring," said Mrs. MacLane.

But Barbara was a normal sixteen-year-old girl. She could not, she simply could not, let a telephone ring without answering, if only long enough to find out who was on the line. She ran into the kitchen and snatched up the receiver with her right hand. She did not dare unclench her left fist even for an instant for fear she might drop the wedding ring. "Hello?" she said breathlessly.

"Hi." It was Bill Cunningham. Of all people. And of all the inconvenient moments for him to call.

"I can't talk," Barbara cried wildly. "We're leaving for the wedding!"

"Yes or no. Bowling tomorrow night?" Bill sounded like a telegram.

"Yes, yes, *yes!*" Barbara hung up and ran out the front door, slamming it behind her. Bill would have to understand. Careful not to sit on her dress, she climbed into the backseat of the car beside Rosemary.

"All set?" asked Mr. MacLane from behind the wheel.

"Barbara, did you remember to try the front door?" asked Mrs. MacLane. "I wouldn't want anything to happen to Rosemary's wedding silver."

"Relax, Mom," said Gordy, who was sitting beside his mother in the front seat.

"Yes, Mother." Barbara was now impatient to start for the church. "I mean I slammed it good and hard."

Rosemary laughed. "I think everybody should stop telling everybody to relax. That's all we've said all day."

Mr. MacLane turned on the ignition and stepped on the starter.

"Who called?" asked Rosemary, who shared Barbara's feelings about ringing telephones.

"Bill Cunningham," answered Barbara, still feeling incredulous. "He's taking me bowling tomorrow night, and I didn't think he would ever call me again. He said he would, but I didn't believe him."

"That's nice." Mrs. MacLane answered automatically.

A mail truck was coming down the street. "Please, let's go before we have to stop and sign for more packages," pleaded Mrs. MacLane.

"Yes," agreed Barbara. "Let's get out of here before something else happens." Bill really had called her. It almost seemed as if she had imagined the call, it had all happened so quickly, but she knew it was real. She also knew that she had learned something about Bill. After this she should take him at his word. His regrets, however jauntily presented, had been sincere after all.

As the MacLanes finally started down the street, the possibility of a flat tire, a most unwelcome thought, popped into Barbara's mind. No, she told herself fiercely, I won't think about such a thing. If I do, it might happen. She fastened her eyes on her nosegay of daisies and tried to think serene, beautiful thoughts appropriate to the spiritual occasion. She thought about how love made Rosemary beautiful, about how cool and fragrant the flowers smelled, and about how kind everyone had been.

"Can't you drive just a little faster?" Mrs. MacLane was plainly nervous.

"It is three forty-seven," said Gordy. "Plenty of time. Don't get in a sweat."

"Not legally," answered Mr. MacLane. "It's less than a five-minute drive to the church. If we drop down to the freeway, we'll make it in plenty of time. Anyway, I imagine Greg will wait a minute or two for Rosemary."

No one spoke as they rode down the winding street toward the freeway. The clock in the tower on the city hall said three forty-nine. Still plenty of time. They approached the railroad track beside the approach to the freeway, and as they started up the incline to cross the track, the signal began to wigwag noisily back and forth, and the black-and-white arm descended in front of the car, blocking their path.

"Dad!" cried Rosemary. "Can't you do something?"

Mr. MacLane glanced at the traffic behind him. It was too late to back up to turn around. Cars had already pulled up behind him. Helplessly the MacLane family sat trapped by the clang-clanging signal.

"Wouldn't you know?" said Barbara. She thought, It's all my fault. If I hadn't stopped to answer the telephone. . . . But if she hadn't answered it, she would have gone off not knowing it was Bill who called.

"I wonder where the train is?" Mrs. MacLane peered down the track. "Oh, here it comes."

The diesel engine honked at the crossroad, and the engineer waved, saw that he was holding up a wedding party, grinned, and waved some more.

No one in the car had the heart to wave back.

"A *freight* train," cried Rosemary in despair.

"Naturally," said Gordy. "Passenger trains don't run on this track anymore."

The freight cars began to click past. Barbara stared at their red and yellow sides as if hypnotized.

" 'Santa Fe all the way,' " Gordy read from the side of a car. " 'Illinois Central, main line of Mid-America.' 'Hydra-cushion for fragile freight.' 'Be specific—ship Union Pacific.' Who do you suppose thinks up these things?"

"It's a mile long." The bride was near tears.

"It can't be. It just seems that way," said her father, as the cars continued to click by. "I think there is a law limiting the length of freight trains."

" 'The Milwaukee, route of the Hiawatha,' " Gordy read on. "And here's 'Santa Fe all the way' again."

Mrs. MacLane had been counting the cars in a dreamlike voice. "Twenty-eight, twenty-nine, thirty. . . ."

" 'Lackawanna, route of Phoebe Snow,' " read Gordy. "Who do you suppose Phoebe Snow is?"

"Maybe she's a friend of Hiawatha, who has his name on the Milwaukee freight cars," suggested Mr. MacLane.

"Mother." The bride sounded frightened. "This is the last time we will all be together. Here, right this minute, with those freight cars going by."

Mrs. MacLane stopped counting to look over her shoulder at her daughter. "We'll be together many times, and Greg will be with us, too."

"But things will be different after I'm married." Rosemary, still frightened, looked wan and defenseless.

The caboose passed, the signal stopped, the black-and-white arm lifted, and the car moved forward onto the approach to the freeway.

"Of course things will be different," answered Mrs. MacLane serenely. "You wouldn't want them to be the same, would you?"

"No . . . no, I wouldn't." Rosemary seemed reassured by the calm in her mother's voice. "Of course I wouldn't."

Two minutes later the car turned off the freeway and drove along the winding street to a little brown church beneath two redwood trees. The trees had been planted too close when the church was new, and now their trunks were crowding the front steps, the branches laced above the entrance. As Barbara stepped out of the car, she could hear the organ playing, and she felt as if she were stepping into a dream. A few guests were hurrying up the steps past the bridesmaids, who were waiting in the vestibule. It was all happening too fast. Gordy had gone into the church, her mother was starting down the aisle on the arm of an usher, the bridesmaids had taken their positions.

Still in a dream, Barbara adjusted the folds of her sister's wedding veil. As her fingers touched the fragile stuff, she discovered a bee crawling inside the lace. It was a lovely bee, yellow and black and furry. Barbara admired it and could not be alarmed. It seemed to be a bee in a dream, it was so beautiful. She lifted the veil and the bee buzzed and flew out, soaring up into the redwood branches that met over the door of the church. It had not been a phantom bee after all. It was a real bee that might have stung the bride. Barbara's hands began to tremble.

Rosemary's radiance had returned. Now it was her father who was nervous. He looked pale and rigid as he stood with his daughter's hand on his arm, as if someone would have to wind him up with a key before he could move down the aisle. Barbara took her place in front of the bride. The organist led into the wedding march. *Here comes the bride.* Anne started down the aisle and then Millie.

Now it was Barbara's turn. As she took her first step on the carpet her nosegay stopped trembling. Her left hand, clenched until it ached, protected Greg's ring, hidden by her flowers. She was calm, moving as rehearsed, seemingly through no will of her own. How serious Greg looked standing beside his brother, and how far away. The aisle of the church had not seemed this long at the rehearsal. The minister looked so . . . welcoming. As she walked, Barbara was aware of faces turned toward her—the smiling Amys with their families, Uncle Charlie's broad round face, her cousin Elinor looking awed, some of Rosemary's college friends. The congregation began to rise, and she knew that eight beats behind her, her

father had got wound up and had started down the
aisle with Rosemary on his arm. Finally in the front
pew, she saw her mother, looking flushed but tran-
quil, while her grandmother wiped away a tear with a
trembling hand.

Barbara took her place and watched Rosemary and
her father moving down the aisle. Rosemary looked so
very young as she smiled at Greg that Barbara felt
frightened for her. This was too big a step for her to
be taking when she barely had the bands off her
teeth. She should have waited until she was older.
Then Rosemary smiled directly at her sister with such
a look of happy confidence that Barbara's misgivings,
although they did not entirely disappear, at least
wavered, and she was able to return the smile.

"Dearly beloved, we are gathered together. . . ." It
seemed to Barbara that their minister was speaking
the familiar words as if they had just been created for
Rosemary and Greg. They were beautiful old-
fashioned words, worn smooth with use, but it seemed
to Barbara she was hearing them for the first time.
Now the father of the bride had given his daughter in
marriage and had stepped back to take his place beside his wife. Barbara had taken her sister's flowers,
and Rosemary's hand was placed in Greg's. It seemed
to Barbara that the ceremony was going much too
quickly. Something so beautiful and important and
binding should last longer. Rosemary's voice was joy-
ful as she spoke her vow, and Greg sounded serious
and . . . reliable, as if, as the older of the two, he
was taking the greater share of the responsibility. She
will always be safe with him, Barbara thought. Then
the minister pronounced Rosemary and Gregory man
and wife. Barbara returned her sister's flowers when
Greg had kissed his bride, and as the swell of the organ filled the church she found herself fairly flying
up the aisle on the arm of the best man. It was over.

Rosemary was married. Behind her nosegay Barbara flexed her fingers, which still ached from the protection she had given the groom's ring.

Suddenly the whole family was in the garden of the church kissing Rosemary. Even Gordy, looking embarrassed, brushed his lips against her cheek without being prodded. Then Mrs. Aldredge and Aunt Josie were taking charge, forming the wedding party into a receiving line. Now the guests were coming out of the church, and Barbara, in her place beside the bride, found herself greeted, kissed, admired. "A beautiful wedding . . . how pretty you look . . . it won't be many years before you . . . such a happy couple . . . a lovely bride, so young . . . you'll be next, my dear. . . ." Barbara nodded and smiled and quite irrelevantly watched for Greg's cousin with the tattooed ears, but she did not see him. He must live in the East.

And then, who should come straggling along at the end of the receiving line, but Tootie Bodger. Barbara did not know why she should be surprised, since he had been included in the invitation to his family. Perhaps because Gordy always tried to escape any social occasion, she expected all boys to be the same way. "Hello, Barbara," he said. And since the line had dwindled and the bridesmaids were drifting away, he added, "You sure look pretty in that blue dress."

"Thank you, Tootie." Barbara smiled, pleased by the compliment and amused to learn that Tootie was color blind. Now she knew why he had come to the wedding. He had come to see her. My woman's intuition tells me, she thought happily.

Tootie stepped aside so that a college friend of Greg's, the one with the beard, who had brought a camera, could take Barbara's picture. The picture was snapped, and the flash bulb was popped into the photographer's hand. He held it out to Mrs. Al who happened to be standing nearby, and said gravely, "Would you care to have this, ma'am? It makes a good darning egg." Without thinking what she was doing, Mrs. Aldredge thanked him, accepted the bulb, and put it in her bag. A moment later she gave him a puzzled look, as if wondering why she should have taken this odd gift.

A character, thought Barbara. There was probably one at every wedding. At least his method of disposing of old flash bulbs was tidier than dropping them in the church shrubbery. She looked around for Tootie, but he was gone. Never mind. He would be back. She was confident of that. It was then that she remembered Bill Cunningham's telephone call. It was the first moment she had had time to think of him since she had started for the church. Yes, yes, *yes,* she had said, an answer that now seemed over-enthusiastic, even though she was eager to go bowling with him. She hoped that Bill would understand this was due to the excitement of the moment.

Rosemary was crossing the lawn to cut her wedding cake. Barbara followed, pausing to write her name in the guest book, presented without a giggle by her cousin Elinor, who was obviously proud of the honor that had been bestowed upon her. "Having fun, Ellie?" she asked.

"Oh, yes," sighed Elinor. "It's a *beautiful* wedding."

Barbara reached the table just as Rosemary was offering Greg the first bite of wedding cake, a moment that the bearded photographer captured before offer-
another darning egg to another puzzled guest.
Barbara felt her Uncle Charlie's arm around her
upon her cheek. "I'll bet you can't wait for
you?" he asked.
now about that," Barbara answered
girl who was willing to go bowling

with a boy, but not mend his shirt. She smiled over
her uncle's shoulder at Rosemary.

"You girls are all alike," said Uncle Charlie. "You
can't wait to get married." He turned to Rosemary as
if expecting her to agree with him.

Rosemary laughed. "You know that's just wishful
thinking, Uncle Charlie. You know you want all the
girls to get married, so their husbands will buy life
insurance from you."

"That's right," agreed Uncle Charlie with a grin,
and then he was serious. "You know what I am going
to do? I am going to give you and your new husband
a twenty-five-per-cent discount on the first year's pre-
miums on any insurance policy you take out. That is
how much I think of you."

Barbara was touched, understanding that her uncle
was offering Rosemary the best he had to give, but
she wondered how Rosemary would react. She need
not have worried. Rosemary kissed her uncle and said,
"Thank you, Uncle Charlie. That's a valuable gift, and
we'll take you up on it." Rosemary loved everyone on
her wedding day.

Barbara drifted on, pausing to speak to Gordy, who
was drinking punch and eating cake alone. "How did
you like the wedding, Gordy?" she asked.

"All right, I guess," he said with his mouth full.
"Only why does a wedding have to make everybody
so kissy all of a sudden?"

"I guess it just does." Barbara laughed and went on
to speak to her grandmother, who was sitting on a
chair someone had brought for her and placed in the
shade of a tree. Gramma smiled and said, "You look
lovely, my dear, and you'll be the next bride in the
family. Mark my words."

"Oh, I don't know about that, Gramma," answered
Barbara. "I have lots of cousins."

Gramma was suddenly serious. She patted her granddaughter's hand and said, "That's right. Don't you be in a hurry. Marriage brings hardships. Believe me, I know. Have a good time while you are young."

"I'm trying to, Gramma," answered Barbara, wondering what memories Rosemary's wedding was bringing back to her grandmother. Her struggles with the old wood stove perhaps and babies when there was not enough money. Barbara thought, too, of that dark hall Rosemary was going to clean as part of her new duties as a landlady and of those four garbage cans lined up under the back stairs.

"You're only young once," Gramma reminded Barbara.

"That's what they tell me," answered her granddaughter, and turned to speak to Millie.

"I had no idea weddings were such fun," said Millie. "I hope I won't be always a bridesmaid, never a bride."

"Bob seems interested," Barbara pointed out.

"I wish I didn't have to go back to Blackfoot so soon." Millie looked a little anxious. After the reception the MacLanes were to take her home to change her clothes and pick up her luggage, before they drove her across the bay to catch the evening train north.

"There's always next semester," Barbara reminded her. "You're sure to meet on the campus and, anyway, you and Bob are more or less kissing kin. You know. The bride's ex-roommate and the groom's brother."

Millie nodded. "That's stretching it a point, but I see what you mean. Maybe the bride and groom will invite us to dinner."

Millie wandered off, and for a moment Barbara stood alone watching the guests. Her father was talking to the minister; her mother, looking a little tired now, was talking to some friends of the Aldredges'.

Tootie and Gordy were drawn together by a mutual feeling of being out of place. Rosemary and Greg and Anne were surrounded by their college friends. Anne was agreeing to going on to San Francisco with some of the crowd. Everyone seemed to be having a good time. The level of the punch bowl had dropped; the cake, which one of the Amys had finished cutting for Rosemary, was almost gone—there might be enough left for the family for supper, if they could remember to take it home. Barbara, knowing she would not be included in the college group going to San Francisco, was beginning to feel left out. There was no place for her to go but home with her family to eat leftover wedding cake. "I know a restaurant out in North Beach that serves *tagliarini al pesto*," someone was saying to Anne, "and we could all go on to that place that has flamenco music."

Greg whispered something to Rosemary. She looked up at him, nodded, and smiled. Barbara felt a twinge of sadness. The wedding was almost over. It had been a lovely wedding, all she had ever dreamed of for her sister. The sun had shone, the flowers were beautiful. . . .

Then Tootie was by her side. "Look, could I drive you home?" he asked. "Mom and Dad said they would go home with friends, so I can have the car." He looked anxious, afraid that she might turn him down with another flimsy excuse.

"I would love a ride home," agreed Barbara, glad to postpone the inevitable letdown after the wedding a while longer. "With the college crowd going off to the city, I was feeling sort of left out."

"Uh . . . I don't know whether you would be interested or not, but there's a folk-song concert over at Hertz Hall tonight. If we drove over now, we could probably get tickets and then have something to eat someplace near the University before the concert."

The apprehension in Tootie's gray eyes told Barbara he was afraid she might not be pleased by his suggestion. She smiled encouragingly. "It sounds like fun, Tootie," she answered. "I like folk songs. I—I've learned quite a few in the past year. But I will have to go home and change my dress first. I can't go over to the University dressed like a bridesmaid."

"Sure," agreed Tootie, relief in his voice. "There's plenty of time."

Why . . . I have dates with two boys for the same weekend, Barbara thought suddenly. Me. The sister of the bride. She was not left out at all. She was beginning to live a life of her own.

Now the word was circulating through the guests that the bride was about to throw her bouquet. Anne took Barbara by the hand. "Come on," she said. "I'm sure all my basketball playing is good practice for this." Smiling back over her shoulder at Tootie, Barbara allowed herself to be led away.

"Where's Millie?" she asked, and found her by the table talking to Bob. "Millie! Come on," she called. "Rosemary is going to throw her bouquet." Millie, too, smiled back over her shoulder at Bob as she joined the girls.

Mrs. Aldredge was taking charge once more. "Why don't you throw it from the steps of the church?" she suggested.

"Good idea." Rosemary ran lightly up the steps and stood facing the gathering beneath the laced branches of the twin redwoods. "Elinor! Where's Elinor?" she asked. "She should have a chance to be the next bride, too."

Blushing with pleasure, the younger girl came through the crowd to join Barbara and the bridesmaids.

"Ready?" Rosemary held up her flowers.

The girls held out their arms as Rosemary tossed

her bouquet toward them. It was Elinor who ran forward and caught the roses and lilies of the valley in her arms. The friends who had gathered to watch laughed affectionately.

"Elinor is going to be the next bride!" cried Rosemary, as Greg came forward and took her by the hand.

For an instant Barbara was disappointed. She had dreamed of catching her sister's bouquet, but when she saw the pure delight shining on Elinor's chubby face her disappointment faded. Along with the roses and lilies of the valley Elinor was welcome to her dreams of being the next bride. That was all it had been—a dream, a childish dream. It was funny, but now that she suddenly had dates with two boys for the same weekend, a lot of things were changed. Life was interesting, something to be explored, and a wedding did not seem nearly so desirable. Tootie and Bill. What a pair. She did not even know which she preferred, Bill's thoughtless exuberance or Tootie's fumbling seriousness. But she did know one thing—it was going to be fun to find out.

Beverly Cleary

YOUNG Love®

IS A VERY SPECIAL FEELING